S0-AQP-670

DATING BLUES

Maud Johnson

SCHOLASTIC INC.
New York Toronto London Auckland Sydney

ISBN 0-590-33462-X

Copyright © 1986 by Maud Johnson. All rights reserved. Published by Scholastic Inc.

12 11 10 9 8 7 6 5 4 3 2   6 7 8 9/8 0 1/9

Printed in the U.S.A.   06

DATING BLUES

A Wildfire Book

WILDFIRE® TITLES FROM SCHOLASTIC

O^{ne}

When you want a special thing to happen but doubt it will, and then it does — it's unbelievable! That's how it was for me with Kenny Chapman. I honestly didn't think he would ever give me a second glance, even though for months I'd secretly ached for him to notice me.

I daydreamed about how marvelous it would be to date him. To date any boy, for that matter. It was hard to be almost sixteen and to never have had a date, especially when most of the girls I knew were going steady. But Kenny was my first choice, with his rugged good looks, and broad shoulders. Kenny with his curly black hair and quick smile.

Kenny couldn't have known that my gazing at his back during history class the week before my birthday had got me into trouble with Mrs. Holmes. She was writing a list of dates on the blackboard, explaining about them at the same time. Instead of listening to what she said, I stared to my left to where Kenny sat two rows over, next to the window. I could see the firm line of his jaw, and his right hand holding a ball-point pen as he copied the dates from the board into his loose-leaf notebook.

". . . . Beth-Ann?"

The sound of my name jarred me and my eyes jerked toward Mrs. Holmes. I realized from her tone of voice that she must have asked me a question. She was glaring in a way that let me know she was aware that I hadn't been paying attention.

"Beth-Ann," she repeated sharply, her lips thinning out, a sign she was annoyed.

Several students turned their heads in my direction. One of them was Kenny. My cheeks felt so hot I knew they had to be bright red.

"I — uh — I didn't — uh — hear the question, Mrs. Holmes," I managed, choking out the words.

The bell signaling the end of class rang before she could speak again. I didn't know if I should stop at her desk and apologize, or ignore the situation. That decision was made for me because by the time I gathered my books together, she was talking with another student. We had only three minutes to change classes and I slipped out into the hall.

Francine Simmons, my best friend, was waiting and fell into step with me. She had been in the history class; her chair was in the front row while mine was in the back. Mrs. Holmes was one of the teachers who assigned seats, or Fran and I would have been sitting together.

"Beth-Ann, what in the world were you doing to make Mrs. Holmes so uptight?" Fran asked.

"Nothing," I shrugged.

"You had to be doing *something*. She sounded as if she'd caught you robbing a bank."

My reply was not a hundred percent the truth. "I was looking out the window instead of at the blackboard and evidently that's a major crime in her eyes."

Fran giggled and I joined in as we went in opposite directions to our next classes. I'd have died before admitting to anybody, even to her, how deeply I felt about Kenny. Being best friends with Fran since we were in grade school had meant sharing lots of secrets over the years, until some months earlier when she began to date. Now, she was going steady with Jack Dayton who, like us, was a high school junior, and all of a sudden an invisible wedge had grown between Fran and me.

Fran believed my not dating was my own fault, that I didn't put myself out enough to attract guys. She seemed unable to realize that I tried. But I couldn't help being shy around boys. Maybe not growing up with brothers was part of it, since I was an only child while Fran had two older brothers who were in college. No matter how much effort

I summoned, I couldn't seem to help the way I was. My mind would have a white-out when I attempted to carry on a conversation with a boy and my hands would turn clammy, things which apparently never happened to Fran.

Once when we were talking about it, after Fran was seeing a lot of Jack but not yet going steady with him, she said, "Beth-Ann, everyone is self-conscious until they're used to dating, but you're making a career out of it. You have to come on to guys a little. Tease them and laugh when they make crazy cracks. You'll never get anyplace with boys if you don't loosen up."

"I just can't think of anything to say," I moaned.

"Oh, for heaven's sake! You can think of plenty to say to me, can't you? Guys don't want you to deliver a lecture. Just make a couple of comments about school or the weather if you can't do better."

I'd deliberately changed the subject, and for a few weeks after that she and I didn't talk about my lack of dates. She hadn't intended to hurt me, although the cut was deep. It didn't help my feelings for my mother to think very much the way Fran did. Mom didn't use Fran's exact words, but her meaning was the same.

When I finished junior high and Mom realized some of my friends were dating, she dropped hints to me. She'd begin a sentence with, "When you're out with boys. . . ." Or she'd ask a question like, "What's the curfew for high school girls these days if it's just a routine date, not a special occasion?" Apparently she expected a line of boys to form outside our house, because when she was a teenager her life had been a whirlwind of good times. She'd been a popular girl with lots of boyfriends. In our attic there were several cardboard boxes of her souvenirs — crepe paper streamers from school dance decorations, corsage ribbons, snapshots of guys, five red satin heart-shaped valentine candy boxes of various sizes, along with other mementos.

It must have shattered her to realize boys paid no attention to me. I knew she didn't deliberately seek to embarrass me by discussing it, but not dating was a special humiliation and talking about it was awful. Usually my mother and I got along well, although as my birthday neared she seemed to be determined that I date the minute I was sixteen, if not before, and she mentioned it until I wanted to scream. A blowup between us was inevitable.

It happened on the first Friday in February, one week before my birthday, a sleety day, with the weather reports hinting of snow before morning. Dad, who was with an insurance firm, came in before Mom did that afternoon and settled in his favorite living room chair with the newspaper. My mother's secretarial job was one of the joys of her life, but she'd apparently had a rough day because she arrived home frowning and muttering that she was delayed leaving the office and then was caught in a rush hour traffic snarl.

I'd already set the table for dinner and was standing at the kitchen sink washing a head of lettuce under running water, then separating the leaves as I'd seen her do countless times. I would have begun cooking if I'd known what she planned to prepare.

"Thanks for doing the salad," she said.

She bustled around the refrigerator, taking out meat and a package of frozen French fries. "Beth-Ann," she said, "we must plan your birthday party for next Friday."

I cleared my throat. "I don't want a party," I answered dryly. "That's kid stuff."

"I don't mean balloons and children's games. But turning sixteen is an important day in a girl's life. In a boy's life, too. You can invite several couples, I've already ordered some refreshments."

"Several couples" — the phrase stabbed me. I would be alone while the others were paired off with dates. No way, I told myself frantically. In a flash I grasped what my mother was thinking: She expected me to invite a boy for myself. Didn't she realize that guys simply didn't find me attractive enough to date?

"Thanks, Mom, but I don't care for a big to-do over my birthday," I said stiffly. "And I especially don't want a party."

The meat patties sizzled in the skillet and she sprinkled them with onion salt. I thought the matter of the party was finished. Was I ever mistaken!

"Well, if you refuse to invite some boys and girls, I'll phone them or ask Fran Simmons to do it for you," she snapped. "Your staying home alone so much is ridiculous and — "

"No!" I cut in.

She wasn't to be stopped. "I've already ordered food, Beth-Ann," she continued, ignoring me as if I hadn't spoken. "Those crunchy cheese pastries from the bakery and a sheet cake. I'll make a sour cream dip for potato chips and — "

"Mom. No!" I exploded, interrupting her again. Jumping up, I raced down the hall into my room and flung the door shut, collapsing facedown on the bed.

How in the world could my mother expect me to approach boys and invite them when no boy had wanted to date me earlier? Boys would make excuses not to come. I knew they would — even Kenny. Besides, I would never find enough nerve to approach Kenny Chapman, and it would be gruesome if Fran arranged a blind date for me under the circumstances — or tried to do it. That would be a public admission that it was impossible for me to get a date on my own.

Our house was small, with the living room in front, then the dining room behind it, and at the rear, the kitchen. Across a short hall were two bedrooms and a bath. I heard Mom's heels clicking as she went from the kitchen into the living room. The door to my room hadn't caught firmly and it eased open about an inch, enough for me to overhear her furious voice as she spoke to Dad.

"I don't know what to do about Beth-Ann!" she stormed.

"What's wrong?" Dad asked.

"I've suggested a party to make her birthday an event for her to enjoy and remember, and she won't even discuss it! At her age she ought to be dating every weekend. But either she baby-sits or is here with us watching TV while all her classmates are out having fun, and that's not normal. Baby-sitting is all right and it's a good way for her to earn spending money, but she shouldn't do it *every* Friday and Saturday. She used to be so sweet and cooperative, but lately, talking to her is like butting my head against a brick wall!"

"Simmer down, Lois." Dad's voice came through my half-opened door as Mom's had, although he spoke more quietly. "You're getting yourself into a stew over this. Kids mature at different ages. Just because Beth-Ann is on the verge of sixteen doesn't mean she's ready for a big-time romance."

"I'm definitely *not* talking about what you call 'a big-time romance!' Good heavens! The girl is too young for anything serious!" Mom's voice was louder than before. "I just mean she ought to have some teenage dates. Francine Simmons dates all the time, that's why she's not in this house as often as she used to be. Beth-Ann's birthday is the perfect opportunity for her to have friends come over, and to get out of that shell she's wrapped around herself. But my attempts to do something nice just make her rude and insulting."

"Honey, you're tired. You'll feel better after you eat and relax a little, so why not drop it for now? If Beth-Ann feels this strongly about not wanting a birthday celebration, the party probably would be a dud anyway."

Mom didn't reply. After a moment Dad said, "What about dinner? I'm starved."

My cheeks were wet with tears, although I hadn't been conscious of crying. Burrowing deeper into the pillow, I tried to stop trembling. My mother's clicking heels told me she was returning to the kitchen.

I could have hugged Dad. For a second I was tempted to run to him and climb on his lap as I used to do when I was small, but I didn't move. You can pull stunts like that if you're six, but not when you're just a week away from being sixteen.

A few minutes later Mom pushed my door all the way open and said, "Dinner is on the table, Beth-Ann."

Without lifting my face from the pillow, I answered that I wasn't hungry.

She came to the side of the bed. "You don't have to eat if you don't want to do it, but you do have to come to the table," she ordered. "Get up and wash your face. And hurry!"

There was no point in my refusing or offering objections because she was using her "you-will-do-it" voice, and I knew she'd insist. I dared not look at my reflection in the bathroom mirror as I splashed cold water on my eyes. Some girls are appealing and pretty when they cry, but I'm not one of them. My eyelids were puffy and my lips trembled. Tears always made my skin blotchy.

The meal was a disaster, not because of the food but from the tension in the dining room. I didn't bother to pick up my knife and fork. Once when I glanced toward Mom, she was cutting her ground beef patty into crumbs without tasting anything on her plate. Dad talked more than usual, as if he was trying to avoid silence or keep Mom from mentioning the party again. Finally, he asked me a question about school and I mumbled a vague answer. When he attempted to draw my mother out about her day, she gave a terse "I don't know," which wasn't like her.

I glanced at Mom again, and realized I'd hurt her feelings.

"Mom, I'm sorry," I said, the words echoing in the still room. "I shouldn't have spoken to you the way I did a while ago. I don't want you to think I don't appreciate your trying to do something for me on my birthday. But it's just — just that I truly don't want a party. I don't want you to be upset, either, or for you to hate me because of it."

Some of the bleakness went out of her eyes and she gave me a quivery smile. "I don't hate you, dear," she answered. "I couldn't hate you if I tried, although I don't like the way you behaved when we were discussing it. I'm disappointed about the party. I'll admit that, because I'll always remember the party my parents had for me on my sixteenth birthday. I had such a lovely time. But it's your happiness that is at stake and if you don't want the party, so be it."

The lump in my throat dwindled until it disappeared. I felt as if a heavy weight had been lifted off my chest, and to my amazement, I realized I was hungry. After trying a mouthful of meat, I nibbled a French fry and ate some of the salad. Everything was delicious.

On Thursday, six days later, I thought about all of it as I sat in study hall at school. The weekend had been routine with Mrs. Cantrell, who lived across the street from us, phoning Saturday morning to know if I'd sit with her two children that night. I was eager to get out of the house in case my mother mentioned the birthday party again. She hadn't referred to it and I decided my birthday must be a dead subject.

Tisha Cantrell was four and her brother Timmy, not quite two. I'd taken care of those youngsters often enough to feel at ease with them. Timmy was in bed when I arrived. After playing with Tisha and reading her a story, I tucked her in and watched television until the Cantrells returned.

Sunday was a do-nothing day for me. Most

of the afternoon was spent studying for a test scheduled on Monday. It was after midnight Sunday when I woke up sick to my stomach. I called Mom about quarter to three in the morning. "I don't know what's wrong," I moaned. "I've been throwing up for two hours and my head hurts. I hurt everywhere."

She took my temperature and said I had a slight fever. An icy washcloth helped my head, and while the nausea stopped after a while, my stomach still felt uneasy. There wasn't a square inch on my body without an ache.

"Two people in my office have had the flu recently," Mom said. "If that's what you have, I hope it's the twenty-four hour kind, so you'll get over it quickly. If you aren't all right when it is time to get up, I'm going to phone Dr. Winters."

"Mom, I have to go to school in the morning. We're having a big math test."

"You can't go anywhere if you're sick. Anyway, I doubt if you could concentrate on a test if you're nauseated and achy and running a temperature, Beth-Ann. Let's wait and see."

At the customary getting-up time Monday morning I still felt achy and miserable. Dr. Winters told Mom my symptoms sounded like a virus that had struck lots of his patients.

"Give Beth-Ann aspirin and plenty of liquids," he advised. "If she's not better Tuesday, bring her to my office."

Mom was right about my taking the math

test; I would have failed it. As bad as I felt, I didn't dwell on school and slept most of the day. During her lunch hour Mom came home to check on me, and I promptly went back to sleep after she returned to work.

What I had must have been the twenty-four hour flu because by evening I was much better. I remained at home Tuesday and went to school on Wednesday. Mr. Dole, the math teacher, was understanding about the test. He said I could make it up after classes Friday afternoon, which meant I'd "celebrate" my birthday by having to stay late at school — something I thought about during study hall Thursday afternoon. The timing wasn't important, I reminded myself. It wasn't as if I'd miss out on any festivities since my birthday promised to be just an ordinary day.

As I sat in study hall Thursday, I mused about the week that was coming to a close. I had no way of knowing that taking the math test, and being late leaving school the next day would make a major difference in my life, and that my birthday would have nothing to do with it.

Two

Breakfast at our house wasn't a sit-down meal on weekdays. As a rule I drank a glass of juice while I was standing at the kitchen counter and then ate cereal or toast; my parents had similar food, plus coffee. None of us was inclined to talk much at that time of day.

It was different on my birthday, though. I was spreading orange marmalade on a slice of toast when Mom came to the kitchen. She gave me a hug and asked if I'd like to open my gifts immediately, or would I rather wait until dinnertime for them.

A tingle of anticipation made me smile. "Now," I answered quickly. "My curiosity will kill me if I have to delay for hours."

Dad, knotting his necktie, joined us and said, "I don't believe I'm old enough to have a sixteen-year-old daughter, Beth-Ann. Maybe we made a mistake in your age and you're actually eleven."

"No way," I came back, and giggled. "It's *sixteen*. Are you afraid somebody will think you're a senior citizen?"

"Well, now that you mention that angle. . . ." He winked at me and we laughed together. My father wasn't forty yet, so no one could accuse him of being ancient.

Mom disappeared into her bedroom and returned with two boxes wrapped in colorful striped paper and tied with satin ribbons, explaining that both were from her and Dad. For the first time I began to feel excited about having a birthday. Being sixteen meant I wasn't a "little girl" any longer. I could get my driver's license and when summer came I could find a real job. Maybe I'd become beautiful overnight, or develop a certain sophistication. . . .

The big box held a white sweater-blouse with a cowl neckline, something I'd been longing for, and the smaller box was a make-up kit. "They're gorgeous, both of them," I beamed at my parents. "Thanks a million."

The math test wasn't as hard as I had anticipated; maybe I was lucky and had studied the right chapters in the textbook. Mr. Dole said he'd correct the paper at once, if I'd like to know how I did without having to wait until Monday. I gave an eager nod. One problem was wrong and my grade was B plus.

Friday morning had been fair although by noon every bit of blue sky was hidden behind thick clouds. Rain began to fall while I was waiting for Mr. Dole to check the test. A few drops splashed down at first, spattering against the classroom windows with a series of *kerplunk!* noises. I hadn't worn a raincoat or brought an umbrella since the sun was shining at breakfast time. I hoped those huge drops would end in a hurry and allow me to get home without being soaked. Our house was seven blocks from school, easy walking distance in good weather, but endless in the rain.

It was four o'clock when I left Mr. Dole and the corridors were deserted. An eerie sensation engulfed me, I'd never been in a school when I didn't see or hear another person. Grabbing my coat and books from my locker, I hurried to the entrance — and swallowed a groan.

Those first droplets had become a hard rain that looked as if it might continue a long time. Mom didn't leave her office until five and I didn't want to have to wait until then. But if I struck out on foot, even running, my coat and shoes would be ruined. I stared through the plate glass doors. Water was already puddling in the school parking lot and the sky was so dark the street lamps had come on, putting circles of murky yellow light on the wet pavement.

Footsteps sounded behind me. Whirling around, I saw Kenny Chapman, of all people.

He was coming toward the door carrying books under one arm and zipping his jacket with his free hand. My heart started to thud against my ribs.

"Hi," he said. "Man, it's really raining, isn't it?"

"Is it ever!" I replied, astonished at answering him in a normal voice.

"You're awfully late leaving school today, Beth-Ann."

I murmured that I'd taken a make-up test. "You're late, too," I added.

"Nope. It's actually early for me. I work for Coach Hardy every afternoon. Usually it's for two or sometimes three hours, but today he just needed me for an hour." Coach Hardy was head of the boys' physical education department.

"What kind of work do you do for him?" I asked, still surprised that Kenny Chapman and I actually were chatting, and that my voice hadn't squeaked.

"Check on equipment. Help clean up the gym, and put team uniforms in the washer and dryer." His mouth twisted into a half-smile. "It's not the greatest job in one sense, but it puts some cash in my pocket, and I like sports. I'd rather be doing this than flipping hamburgers in a fast food joint."

I couldn't think of a logical remark to keep the conversation going and was silent. Kenny shifted his books from one arm to the other.

"This rain has set in for the night, so I think I'll make tracks," he announced. He pushed his shoulder against the plate glass door, paused and glanced back at me. "Do you have a ride, Beth-Ann?"

I shook my head.

"Look, I'll give you a lift." He went on, "My car's at the far end of the parking lot, so you wait here and I'll drive up for you. My jacket is waterproof, but your coat doesn't look like it is."

My heartbeats were so loud in my ears, it's a marvel he didn't hear them. I thanked him, and couldn't believe what I said next.

"Let me hold your books, Kenny. You can run faster without them and you know how messy paper is when it's wet."

He thrust the two books and looseleaf notebook at me, and our fingers touched for a split second. I was dazzled, as if fireworks were exploding on every side. I was holding Kenny Chapman's books and he was going to drive me home! Me — Beth-Ann Hughes! The realization spun round and round in my brain. I knew how Cinderella felt when her fairy godmother appeared to turn her ragged clothes into a ball gown and the pumpkin into a glittering coach.

Kenny's car was a blue Ford that looked several years old. He braked at the foot of the school steps and I slid in beside him. I lay his books on the seat between us but held tightly to my books, as if clutching them against my body would help me to breathe normally. I gave him directions to my house.

Then, what I dreaded happened: My mind went blank.

I couldn't think of anything to say except to mention the weather and we'd already discussed that. Visibility was so poor Kenny leaned forward, straining to see through the windshield as he inched the car along. I hoped his silence was an indication he needed to concentrate on driving, not that he was so bored being with me he wasn't bothering to talk.

Did he regret offering me a ride? I wondered about it. He lived in the opposite direction, so he was going out of his way to bring me home. Some weeks earlier I'd looked up his address in the telephone directory after seeing the front of his notebook where he'd printed *Kenneth A. Chapman, Jr.* in block letters amid a lot of doodling. The "junior" had made it easy to know which Chapman his father was. I'd had no intention of phoning him, but I relished any tidbits of information.

"Second house from the corner on the right," I said, as we reached my block.

"Nice place, Beth-Ann. Gray and white is a great color scheme."

Maybe his liking my house gave me courage. I don't know. But I was conscious of not wanting the ride to end, of not wanting to leave his car and have him drive away. I was afraid I'd never see him again, except in class.

"Kenny, would you like to come in for a Coke?" I asked.

If he had waited even half a minute to reply, I'd have died on the spot, but he spoke quickly and grinned at the same time. "Sounds good," he said.

Hard rain continued to come down and we got wet once more as we hurried to the house. I didn't mind; I seemed to be floating rather than putting my feet on a hard surface. Once we were inside, I brushed water from the top of my head and laughed as Kenny remarked that he needed to "shake like a dog." We spread our damp coats on chairs to dry and took seats at the kitchen table facing each other with our Coke cans and a plate of cheese and crackers between us.

Our conversation was mostly about school — it might be more accurate to say he talked and I listened. It turned out he liked math and detested history, which bothered me a little since history is my favorite subject. I discovered he had a thirteen-year-old brother named Judd and that his blue Ford had belonged to his grandfather, who was forced to stop driving because of poor eyesight.

We were still sitting at the kitchen table when my mother came home from work. She looked dumbfounded, and the reason was obvious to me. I'm positive the last thing she expected was to find me there with a boy.

"Mom, this is Kenny Chapman," I said, and that time my voice did squeak.

Kenny stood up to acknowledge the introduction, and I knew his doing it impressed Mom, as she had a big thing about manners.

He looked at his watch, commenting that he hadn't realized it was late, then right in front of my mother he said, "How about seeing a movie tonight, Beth-Ann?"

He was asking me for a date! The room began to spin before my eyes. I was suddenly terrified that I wouldn't be able to say a word and he would assume I didn't want to go, so I nodded.

Mom disappeared into another part of the house and I found my voice. "I'd like that," I managed hoarsely.

"Great. Okay to pick you up at seven?"

Anything would have been okay. I nodded again. Smiling at him was the easiest thing I'd ever done in my life.

As soon as Kenny left my mother came out of her room. "He seems like a very nice boy," she said, emphasizing "very."

He is. Oh, he is. I thought, without speaking aloud.

"Did you meet him at school?" she inquired.

Mumbling, "Yes," I drew a deep breath and blurted out, "I'm going to the movies with him tonight," and ran to my room to get ready.

Having a date was such a new experience for me I didn't know what to expect — by quarter to seven there were butterflies in the bottom of my stomach. I assumed Kenny would go straight from my house to the movie, instead, he drove to a big shopping mall where we wandered around for more than an hour. Other kids were doing the same thing and we saw a few people from our school, but not anyone he or I knew well. Conversation was difficult, for me, anyway. If I hadn't been able to comment on displays in the shop windows, I might not have spoken at all.

Shortly before nine we returned to his car and headed for the theater. A new worry gnawed at me. I wondered how to react if he put his arm around me when we were watching the picture, or if he'd try to hold my hand. I wanted him to do both yet I didn't want him to. Just thinking about it made my palms perspire, and no boy wanted to hold a damp, cold hand.

As things turned out, my fears proved to be useless as Kenny seemed more intent on eating a box of popcorn and looking at the screen than touching me.

The movie was a long one and didn't end until almost twelve. "Do you have to be home by a certain time?" he asked, as we left the theater.

"I — uh — by midnight." That was a lie, Mom hadn't given me a definite time. But Fran had to be in by twelve, and from the way Kenny asked the question, I had the feeling he assumed I had a curfew.

"Then I guess we shouldn't stop for something to eat, Beth-Ann."

I wished instantly I'd told him I could stay

out forever. It wasn't that I was hungry, but I didn't want the evening to end. Just to be saying something, I commented that the popcorn had filled me up — a joke of a statement as he'd eaten most of the box.

"We'll take a raincheck on food," he told me. "We could get together tomorrow night if you want."

If I wanted. I caught my breath. He was asking me for another date! My heart was thumping like a bongo drum and I couldn't stop smiling as I told him Saturday night would be super.

The rain became a drizzle, the windshield wipers lazily swished back and forth across the glass, instead of moving at top speed as they had previously. Kenny turned on the car radio and I hummed along with the music to save myself from trying to think of something to say. But in the back of my mind another worry was forming: Would he expect a good-night kiss? How would I know? I had never kissed a guy my own age. Was there a special technique to be used whenever a boy and girl kissed?

I was borrowing trouble, and like my earlier fear, this one was unnecessary. Kenny stopped the car, walked me to the porch and said, "See you tomorrow night, Beth-Ann. Seven again? Want to go out for pizza?"

"Sure," I replied quickly. I'd have given the same answer if he'd suggested our eating gravel.

The instant my key turned in the lock, he bounded down the steps. His car door slammed shut and he zoomed off.

Inside the house, I stood very still for a minute, hugging my arms across my body, trying to get my breathing back to normal. Lights burned in our living room, although nobody was in sight, so apparently Mom was listening out for me. She came from her bedroom wearing a robe over her nightgown, a bright, expectant smile on her face.

"Did you have a good time?" she asked.

Her voice was filled with anticipation and I realized she'd like me to recount every second of the evening. The strange part was that I wanted to talk about my date, but not to her, and the feeling didn't make sense. I'd have phoned Fran if it hadn't been so late.

"Yes. A good time," I murmured. " 'Night, Mom."

"Wait a minute, Beth-Ann! Will you see Kenny again soon?"

"Tomorrow." I added another good-night. I'd have had to be blind not to notice the excitement in her eyes.

"You see!" she exclaimed. "I told you all you needed was to loosen up with boys! If you'd agreed to the party, Kenny could have been your date!"

I let that slip by unanswered, knowing I could never have invited Kenny or any boy unless he approached me first. It was one truth my mother seemed unable to understand.

Three

On weekends I usually slept late unless I had something special to do. It was past ten o'clock when I woke up the morning after Kenny's and my first date. Pale, wintry sunshine came through the bedroom windows and I snuggled under the covers, reliving the previous day. I was unable to shake my astonishment that Kenny had offered me a ride home and asked me for a date, and even more stunned by his wanting to be with me again.

Suddenly I felt different. It wasn't something I could explain, since nothing happened during the date to change me, but overnight I truly had changed. I was more confident — happier. Maybe it wasn't merely having a date, I told myself; being sixteen was also part of it. I even wondered if I looked different, and hopped out of bed to cross the room to the bureau and stare at my reflection in the mirror.

On the outside I was the same Beth-Ann Hughes, with the same light brown hair and hazel eyes I'd always had. Yet inside there was a new me. I wasn't stupid enough to think I would instantly develop a marvelous personality or gorgeous looks. I knew I'd probably have the same old problem keeping a conversation going with a boy, too. But I figured I must not be as much of a dud as I'd feared if a boy like Kenny Chapman was taking me out on two consecutive evenings. I smiled at the girl in the mirror and she returned the smile. Dating, just one date, made me radiant.

Still wearing my pajamas, I went to the kitchen and found a note from Mom saying she and Dad had gone to the supermarket. That meant I could call Fran without an audience, since our phone was in the living room. I balanced a bowl of cereal on my knees while I was dialing the Simmons house. Fran's hello sounded sleepy.

"Guess what I did last night?" I blurted out. She and I always recognized each other's voices and didn't need to identify ourselves.

"Whatever it was must have been fantastic," she replied. "You seem to be on cloud nine."

"I am! Guess who took me to the movies?"

"Beth-Ann, was it a guy? You had a date?" Wide-awake now, she actually squealed. "Who was he? Do I know him? When did all of this happen? Is — "

"Hold it!" I cut in and giggled. "Yes, you know him, but how can I tell you if you won't be quiet?"

"Okay, I'll hush. Who?"

I decided to tease her by dragging it out. "Well, he has curly black hair and — "

"Who?" she demanded.

"Kenny Chapman."

Her gasp was audible over the phone. I giggled again.

"You've been holding out on me, Beth-Ann!" she said in an accusing tone. "When did all of this happen? Kenny, no less. I thought he was dating Vicki Burt. Jack and I saw them together at the movies a couple of weeks ago, but they must not be going steady if he dated you last night."

The mention of Vicki Burt made a cold shiver go up my backbone because she was a pretty, popular girl at school. I knew her casually and had no idea she and Kenny had ever dated. But then, I hadn't been in the habit of keeping tabs on my classmates, except the ones who were so wildly in love that knowledge of their romances was public information.

Fran was full of questions and I told her what had happened Friday afternoon and evening.

"And you're dating him again tonight?" she asked as soon as I was quiet. "You must have wowed him. How many times did he kiss you?"

My face felt hot, and I was glad she couldn't see me blush. "He — uh — he didn't," I said.

"Not even when he told you good-night? Didn't he try?"

The heat in my cheeks became a scorching burn. "I — I — " Swallowing hard, I asked her a question. "Fran, how do you tell if a boy wants to kiss you?"

"You just know. It's instinct, I guess. You gave him a chance, didn't you? I mean, you didn't just dash into the house and leave him waiting, I hope."

Had I done that? I wasn't sure. "I don't think I did," I told her. "What do you mean by 'giving him a chance'?"

"Honestly, Beth-Ann! How can you be so dumb? You sound like you live in a vacuum. I'm talking about encouraging him. When Kenny brought you home, did you let him know you'd like to be kissed? You did want it to happen, didn't you?"

"How could I let him know? I certainly wasn't about to make an announcement, Fran. It was raining and — " I broke the sentence off, feeling more miserable by the second. Fran implied it was my fault that there were no kisses, just as in the past she felt it was completely my fault I didn't have any dates.

"I don't care about the weather. It could have been hailing golf balls," she replied. "If a boy wants to kiss you, and you want to be kissed — for heaven's sake make it easy for him! Stand close to him and part your lips ever so slightly — that gives him a clue. Lean toward him a little. Did you invite him to come in your house?"

"I couldn't. It was midnight."

"When you told him you enjoyed the date, did you look at his mouth? Even if you did nothing but stand there and smile, he'd get the message. Are you sure you gave him a chance?"

"I'm not sure at all," I sighed.

"Then change your tactics tonight. That is, if you want to keep dating him. Boys don't go much for the ice-water treatment."

"If I'd been a complete icicle, would Kenny have asked me for a date tonight?" I came back. Fran had put me on the defensive and I was standing up for myself.

"I guess he wouldn't. Tonight you — " She paused, and I could hear her talking to somebody in the room with her. "Beth-Ann, my mother needs to use the phone, so I'll have to hang up," she said. "Want to do something this afternoon?"

"Sure."

"I'll phone you around lunchtime and we'll make some plans. 'Bye for now."

The line went dead and rang again instantly. This time it was Mrs. Cantrell.

"Thank goodness I found you at home, Beth-Ann," she said. "Will you stay with Tessa and Timmy tonight?"

I'd never refused her before and it seemed odd to say, "Not tonight, Mrs. Cantrell. I'm sorry."

"Oh, dear. I should have contacted you earlier, but Richard and I didn't decide to go out for dinner tonight until a little while ago, and your line has been busy this morning. Do you have another baby-sitting job tonight?"

"No." I drew a long breath. "I have a date."

Her oh showed her surprise. Maybe she thought she'd never hear me make that statement.

"I can't ask you to change your plans." She went on in a hesitant way. "Does this mean you won't do any more baby-sitting in the future? My children love you and I feel very safe leaving them when you're on the scene."

"I'll still baby-sit, Mrs. Cantrell, but tonight it's not possible. Try me again."

She assured me she would. I almost felt as if I'd lied to her when I put the phone down, because if Kenny and I should go steady — if — naturally we would date every weekend. I hoped desperately it would happen. As much as I liked the Cantrell youngsters and liked earning money baby-sitting with them, dating Kenny was my first priority.

That afternoon Fran and I went to a shopping center and wandered around as Kenny and I had done the previous night. While we talked about many topics, we always came back to the subject of boys. Fran had been going steady with Jack Dayton since January and she loathed the fact that on Saturdays he had an all-day job at a dry cleaning firm, which meant she didn't see him until night.

When we tired of walking, we found a bench in the enclosed mall. "Are you in love with Jack?" I asked. I'd never asked her that question before, because it hurt too much to discuss somebody else's relationship with a boy when I was dateless. Going out with Kenny must have made me bold.

"I guess I am." She gave a shrug.

"Don't you know, Fran?"

"Sometimes I think it would be fun to date a bunch of guys rather than being tied to one. But don't get me wrong, Jack is tops. He's *numero uno* in my book. It's all or nothing with him, though. He says he won't date me if he has to share me with other guys. And going steady does have some advantages; I don't have to worry about whether or not I'll be sitting home alone waiting for the phone to ring."

I turned my head away, not wanting her to see my face. I knew all about sitting home praying a boy would phone, waiting and waiting for something that didn't happen.

"I do like Jack a lot," she confided. "It's just that doing the same old stuff all the time gets boring. I don't know what kind of action I want, but. . . . Oh, well. . . ." She seemed engrossed in pulling a dangling thread off the hem of her jeans and didn't bother to finish whatever she'd been about to say. Later I was to remember her comment, although it wasn't important at the time she made it. I was too full of my own hopes and plans to dwell on her and Jack.

An early twilight was setting in as we left the mall. She asked what Kenny and I planned to do that night.

"He mentioned pizza," I answered.

She shook her head. "Jack is the only person I know who doesn't like pizza. He dotes on spaghetti and ravioli, but can't abide pizza, and it doesn't make sense to me. Kenny will probably take you to Monty's, and pizza is the only food they serve there. Maybe we'll bump into you two later in the evening. What will you do after you eat?"

"I don't know. He didn't say."

I didn't add that I wanted Kenny all to myself. That in the future after he and I had dated a lot — *if* we dated a lot — we could plan something with another couple, but not yet. Thank you, Jack, for not liking pizza, I thought silently.

Kenny was prompt, coming on the dot of seven. He gave me an appreciative glance that made me glow all over. On Friday I'd worn jeans with my new birthday sweater for our date and didn't want to use the same outfit twice on successive nights. On Saturday I was wearing a cranberry-colored skirt with a silky, white blouse.

"You look good," he said softly, as we got

into his car. "Smell good, too. I like girls who use perfume."

Smiling at him, I vowed silently to use perfume forever.

As Fran surmised, we went to Monty's, a restaurant popular with teenagers. The place was more rustic than fancy; the brown walls were decorated with posters of Italian scenes, and the square tables topped with a red plastic finish. The lights were dim and a sound system played popular songs. The music was low enough for us to talk without having to shout. The menu consisted solely of soft drinks and forty different kinds of pizza.

We had just taken our seats when Whit Markham came into the restaurant with Vicki Burt. Kenny jumped up, motioning for them to join us. I froze, my smile instantly as plastic as the shiny finish on the tables. Whit, a tall, heavy-set fellow with white-blond hair, was a friend of Kenny's, something I already knew, since they were together a lot at school.

Vicki disconcerted me because she was so pretty and vivacious I felt plain in contrast. She was a tiny girl, not much over five feet tall, with a perfect figure and reddish gold hair curling softly around a heart-shaped face. Her huge blue eyes had a built-in sparkle, matching her blue sweater and slacks.

"Hope we didn't keep you guys waiting," Whit said, and his remark made me guess the boys must have planned to meet at Monty's, even though Kenny hadn't mentioned it to me in advance. Had Vicki known? For some reason, I felt she did. A rush of disappointment engulfed me as I felt that my evening with my date was about to be ruined.

I couldn't have been more mistaken.

We didn't talk about serious stuff; a lot of silly cracks were tossed back and forth, and all of us laughed often. Vicki, despite her attractiveness, didn't monopolize the conversation, and I forgot to be self-conscious and found myself chiming in.

As we finished eating Vicki said, "Why don't we adjourn to my recreation room? Our chairs are a little more comfortable than these, and if you want to take off your shoes there, feel free."

"Good suggestion," Kenny replied. "I second the motion. All in favor say, 'Aye.' "

There was a chorus of ayes and a man at the next table called, "I don't know what your voting for, but count me in." That made us chuckle. None of us knew him, but he gave us a salute as we left Monty's.

Kenny and I followed Whit's car from the restaurant parking lot past the high school, to the suburban area where the Burts lived. A quarter moon was rising, bright gold in the dark sky. Kenny gave me a sideways glance and said, "There's enough space between us for two people, Beth-Ann. Why don't you slide over nearer me — that is, unless you don't like the idea."

I thought my heartbeats would crack my

ribs, and I couldn't think of anything to say as I moved closer.

"That's better," he whispered, and grinned. "Don't you think so?"

"A lot better," I managed shakily. I'd never been that close to a boy before. Our sides were touching, and the warmth from his body seeped into mine. For once, silence seemed appropriate, and neither of us spoke the rest of the way.

Vicki's house was a long, one-story brick ranch with many windows, and a curving walk from the street to the front door. We entered a vestibule, and while we were taking off coats her mother came in and greeted the boys as if she knew both of them well. Vicki introduced me, and for a split second I felt like an outsider, but the sensation vanished with Mrs. Burt's cordial warmth. Like Vicki, she had the knack of putting everyone at ease.

The recreation room was at the back of the house — a rectangular area with pine-paneled walls and colorful, striped draperies. A Ping-Pong table stood at one end and at the other, a log fire burned on the hearth that was flanked by two red sofas with big, squashy cushions. It was, I decided, the most inviting room I'd ever seen.

Vicki asked if we'd like to watch TV or play a game. When nobody responded, she and Whit sat on one sofa while Kenny and I were opposite them on the other. After a while Whit took a fresh log from the woodbox and put it in the fireplace. We watched the crimson flames shoot up, and somehow it wasn't necessary to chatter every minute as we'd done at Monty's. We did talk, though. Afterwards, I couldn't recall much that was said. I just knew it was a lovely evening.

At half past eleven Kenny and I left. Stepping outside in the cold air, I automatically reached into my coat pocket for gloves. He startled me by taking the gloves, and returning them to my pocket.

"I'll keep your hands warm," he whispered, and his fingers curled around mine. "Darn it, I can only hold one of your hands if I'm going to drive."

"I know how to remedy that." I surprised myself by answering effortlessly, pretending to be serious. "You can hold my left hand half the way to my house and my right hand the rest of the distance."

"Brilliant solution, Beth-Ann. You're a smart girl. You'll make your mark in the world."

Both of us laughed and I sat even closer to him in the car than I had during the ride from Monty's.

I knew he wanted to kiss me good-night, knew it instinctively just as Fran told me I would, and a fluttery sensation swept over me. But when we turned the corner I swallowed a groan. Mom had left the porch light burning, and the entrance to our house was as bright as day.

Kenny wouldn't kiss me under that white

glare — no boy would. I almost burst out crying.

"Your folks must own the power company to use all that electricity," he mumbled.

"I — I — " I had no answer. Finally I said, "Nothing like that." I was dying slowly as I walked beside him up the steps. The house key was in my hand.

"Can I come in with you, Beth-Ann? Just for a minute."

My throat tightened. I tried to speak and couldn't. But I looked at him and he must have read *yes* in my face, for he followed me into the living room. A lamp on the table next to the sofa was on, but because of its opaque shade, the light was soft, and neither Mom nor Dad was in evidence.

Kenny eased the front door shut behind us without making any noise. I found myself leaning against it facing him, the knob cutting into my spine. He put his hands on my shoulders. Maybe I parted my lips the way Fran said a girl should, I don't know. We didn't speak to each other and for some unknown reason, I couldn't meet his eyes. His breath was warm on my cheek and I felt myself being pulled away from the door and against the hardness of his chest until his mouth covered mine.

When the kiss ended I gasped, reeling, and he kissed me again. My eyes had been closed, although I didn't realize it until I had to will myself to open them. Everything blurred as if I was seeing him through a mist.

"I'd better make tracks," he whispered.

Don't go yet — don't go yet — don't go. I begged silently, knowing he should leave before one of my parents came into the room.

"Kenny . . . ." My voice was so faint I barely heard myself.

"Mmmm?"

"Tonight has been fun."

"I think so, too. I wish we could be together tomorrow."

Panic at the idea of not seeing him Sunday made me ache. All of a sudden it was difficult to breathe.

"Can't we?" I asked.

He shook his head. "My grandfather will be eighty years old on Tuesday of next week, and my parents, Judd, and I are going to North Carolina tomorrow to spend the day with him in an early birthday celebration. We're bringing presents, and Mom has cooked a roast and decorated a cake."

"Where in North Carolina?"

"Raleigh."

At last I was able to meet Kenny's eyes. The mist had cleared, and my vision was normal once more. I could see the dimple in his chin, and make out the dark hairs of his eyebrows.

"Maybe you could stay here," I suggested.

"I feel obligated to go, Beth-Ann. After all, Grandpa gave me the car; I wouldn't have wheels otherwise. I can't even promise to phone you tomorrow night, worse luck, because we probably won't get home until real late. But I'll see you at school Monday."

Leaning forward, he kissed me again.

My first kiss . . . kisses — in the plural. After Kenny's car was out of sight around the corner, I bolted the front door and turned off the living room lamp. I tiptoed across the hall as quietly as possible, in the hope that neither of my parents would speak to me. They didn't, although I'd have bet any amount Mom was still awake.

It took a long time for me to fall asleep. I was quivery with excitement and at first I lay on my back, then turned toward the window. The moon was a silvery color rather than the warm gold Kenny and I had noted earlier. Its glow put enough light in my room for the furniture to be outlined darkly against the pale blue walls.

Touching my mouth with my fingers, I relived the kisses, aware that remembering made my heart beat very fast. I had believed I knew how it would feel for a boy to put his arms around me and kiss me, but my wildest daydreams weren't as delicious as actually having it happen. Kenny must like me a lot to kiss me more than once, I mused, smiling in the dim room. I'd been worried I wouldn't know how to kiss, but the fear was silly. When the time came I knew.

$F\underline{our}$

I didn't rush to get up Sunday morning. The sky was overcast without a trace of sunshine, and it was pleasant to linger in bed remembering Kenny's delicious kisses. I could still feel his lips on mine, feel how warm his arms were as he folded them around me. For what seemed the millionth time, I wished he could be in Richmond with me and not in North Carolina.

Had he and his family left home early enough for them already to have reached Raleigh? The clock on my bedside table showed thirteen minutes before ten o'clock. I wasn't sure of the exact number of miles between Richmond and Raleigh, but knew it was about a three-hour drive. Were Kenny and his brother sightseeing? I doubted it, not when the visit was special, for their grandfather's birthday. They'd have to postpone what Kenny called "the tourist bit" until another trip.

After half an hour I slipped into a quilted housecoat and went to the kitchen. Dad was out somewhere, and Mom, who also had on a robe, sat on a high stool at the counter reading the newspaper, and drinking coffee from her favorite ceramic mug. She must have been baking, since a spicy scent filled the kitchen.

"Well, hello," she said and smiled in my direction. "I was beginning to wonder if you planned to sleep all day. Want breakfast?"

"Just juice for now. Something smells good."

"I made a carrot cake. It's from a mix, but I understand it's good. It has to bake another twenty minutes."

Taking a carton of orange juice from the refrigerator, I filled a glass and carried it to the counter, perching on a stool beside Mom. Eventually she'd ask about my Saturday night date, I knew that for certain, but I didn't think she'd bombard me with questions at once. I was mistaken.

"Did you and Kenny have a nice time last night?" she asked.

"A real good time."

"He's a very attractive boy." Her bright, expectant expression was an invitation for me to tell her about the evening. When I was silent, she said, "What did you do after you ate?"

I mentioned our meeting Vicki and Whit.

At that moment something amazing happened to me — I began to talk and couldn't stop. It was as if I was gabbing with another sixteen-year-old girl, and not to my mother. I told her about the pizza restaurant, going to Vicki's house, and described the recreation room with its red sofas and huge fireplace. The only part I didn't report was Kenny's and my kisses.

With an unanticipated suddenness, the feelings inside me changed again. Mom and I were no longer two girls the same age. *I* was still a teenager, but she'd become my mother once more. I couldn't explain to myself why it happened. I just knew we'd returned to our old relationship.

"Mom, Vicki is truly lucky to have that recreation room. The furniture isn't just pretty, it's sooo comfortable." I drew the word out. "The room is at the back of the Burts' house, which lets Vicki and her friends make a lot of noise there if they want without bothering anyone in the living room up front."

Finishing my juice, I added wistfully, "I wish we had two living rooms. There would be one for you and Dad, and one where I could — " I was about to say, "where I could date," and caught myself. "One for my friends," I murmured.

It dawned on me that I must sound as if I'd been dating for ages. Apparently I'd already forgotten being the girl who refused to have a birthday party because she'd have to invite boys, and about not having had any dates until two days previously. Kenny's attention was giving me new self-confidence.

"I wish we did, too," my mother said. "In the past, this house has been adequate for the three of us, but now . . . I suppose. . . ." She left the sentence dangling.

"I love this house, Mom. I don't want us to move, don't get me wrong on that. But couldn't we add a room? It might take up most of the backyard, but we don't use the yard a lot. Couldn't we?"

Her reply came too quickly. "I'm afraid not. Not right now."

"Why not? You and Dad get the things you want. So for once, why can't you do what I want?" Disappointment made my voice shrill. "I really need a recreation room! I think you're acting selfish to say no without even thinking about it!"

Her back stiffened when I said selfish, and she cupped both her hands around the yellow mug as if clutching it might give her extra support.

"We're saving every penny toward your college education, Beth-Ann," she answered. "Adding on even just one room is expensive."

"But college is a year and a half away! I'm only a junior!"

"The time will be here before you know it."

An ugly, raw anger boiled inside of me. A recreation room was somehow as vital to me as breathing, and I felt I'd die if she didn't approve it.

"You've been bugging me to invite people here, and it's no fun if you and Dad are hovering around my friends all the time!" I burst out. "I can't even have a telephone conversation without one of you listening to every word, because with the phone in the living room, there's no such thing as privacy in this house!"

If I'd slapped her, she couldn't have appeared any more shocked. The eager, expectant expression she'd had when she asked about my date had vanished, and frown lines made horizontal marks across her forehead. Sliding off the counter stool without speaking, she went to the stove and opened the oven door, sending a blast of heat surging into the kitchen as she removed the cake.

The room was painfully silent. Embarrassed by what I'd said and the way I'd spoken, I realized how unkind I must have sounded in accusing her and Dad of being selfish.

"Mom —" The harshness was out of my voice, and I wondered if I looked as guilty as I felt.

"Perhaps we can put an extension phone in your room," she said. She was icily calm, and I knew from experience it was a front to mask her real feelings. "I'll talk to your father about it when he comes in."

"Oh, Mom —"

"It won't be a private line, Beth-Ann. Just another phone with our number. But you'll be able to talk to your friends without an audience."

She was so understanding I felt more remorseful than ever. Tears came into my eyes, and I blinked to make them go away, not succeeding completely.

"Mom, I didn't mean what I said a minute ago about your being selfish, or about Vicki being lucky because of the Burts' recreation room. Honest, I didn't. I'm lucky, too. You and Dad are awfully good to me."

It was an apology and I hoped she'd know I was attempting to say I was sorry. Ironically, uttering the words didn't make me feel much better, or ease my inner turmoil. I knew I'd hurt her deeply.

"I — I don't mean to — to blow up at you all the time," I went on in a quivery voice. "I don't know why I'm so spiteful lately, especially when you're trying to do what you think is best."

"Oh, my dear." She hurried across the kitchen to put one hand on my arm and her other hand under my chin, lifting my face to hers.

"I suspect it's part of your growing up," she said gently. "Some of it is my fault because I'm having to learn that I can't give you orders the way I used to do when you were younger." Her fingers were light on my arm, but my flesh seemed to burn from the touch.

"Beth-Ann, my mother and I had fierce

arguments when I was in my teens and I haven't forgotten them." She went on, "I can't recall what we fought about, only that there were times when I hated her and she probably felt the same about me. If it will make you feel better, those reactions passed and once I was older, she and I became friends again. I realize now that the arguments were as hard on her as they were on me. And I promised myself back then if I ever had children, I wouldn't let it happen. But it's happening, just the same."

"Oh, Mom — "

"Perhaps if you and I are more patient, and try harder to see one another's point of view, we can cope."

I wanted to speak, but couldn't. Suddenly, I buried my face in her shoulder the way I used to do when I was small and needed comforting. After I had myself under control enough to raise my head, tears were shining in her lashes. They hadn't rolled down her cheeks as mine did, but they were there.

That February afternoon seemed endless to me. I guess the good times Friday and Saturday nights with Kenny made being alone all the more grim.

After lunch I phoned Fran, learning from her mother that she'd gone out with Jack. I toyed with the idea of phoning Vicki, but vetoed it since I didn't know her well. Until the previous evening, I had never been around her except to say hello at school, and my old shyness caused me dread being considered pushy by trying to latch on to a popular girl. Calling Vicki would have been futile anyway, I rationalized. No doubt she was with Whit or some other boy; from what I'd heard at school, she didn't go steady but she dated lots of different guys.

Besides, I reminded myself wryly, Mom and Dad — and our phone — were in the living room. My parents would be there for hours, since Dad was watching an afternoon sports program on TV. And our television set, like the phone, was located in the living room.

With nothing better to do, I began a book that I needed to write a report on for English, settling down on my bed with the pillows pushed behind my back. But despite the teacher's claim that the book was a literary classic, it was dull reading. My mind strayed — to Kenny — to Mom, and our morning conversation in the kitchen — to Dad, saying while we ate lunch that he would see about an extension phone for my room — to Kenny once more.

About four o'clock, streaks of pale sunshine pushed through the gray clouds and I decided to walk to a convenience store several blocks away for a package of notebook paper. I hadn't actually run out of paper, although a fresh supply would be needed soon. But I was restless, the walls of my room were closing in on me.

The outside air was cold, and there was

enough wind to swirl my hair around my face. I wished I'd brought a scarf and was thankful for the gloves that were in my coat pocket, remembering as I put them on how Kenny removed them from my hands Saturday night.

Not many people were on the street. A few cars passed; I saw three joggers, and waved to old Mr. and Mrs. Simpson, who took an afternoon walk every day regardless of the weather. In our section of Richmond the houses weren't large or fancy, but residents took pride in keeping their property in good condition. Trees lined the sidewalks, and during summer, the yards were always bright with flowers, and lovely green grass. In contrast, everything looked drab that February day. The bare tree branches formed dark, stick-like silhouettes against the sky, and even the evergreens appeared rusty.

There was only one person I knew in the convenience store, Chris Abernathy. He's a tall guy with dark red hair who played left end on the high school football team, and who was in some of my classes. He was leaving, coming through the plate glass doors as I arrived, and each of us said hello at the same instant. I didn't linger in the store. The sun was disappearing behind some misty clouds once more and darkness would come early. I walked very fast as I headed home.

My house was in view when a car braked beside me and a familiar voice said with a laugh, "We'd offer you a ride, Beth-Ann, but I don't know where you'd sit."

It was Mrs. Cantrell, and before she finished speaking Tessa piped up with "Beth-Ann, Beth-Ann" in her little girl singsong voice. They were in their Volkswagen, Mr. Cantrell driving, his wife in front beside him while Tessa, Timmy, and the dog, Columbus, filled the backseat. Columbus, a mixture of many breeds, was larger than either of the children.

"Thanks. But I don't know where I'd sit either, unless I climbed on the hood," I replied, and giggled. "Anyway, I'm practically home."

They knew that, of course. The Cantrell house was diagonally across the street from us.

"Are you free tonight?" Mrs. Cantrell asked. "Since we didn't go out last night, when we turned the corner and saw you we had simultaneous brainstorms about going somewhere tonight."

I said I was available, and she added, "We won't be late coming in. Tell that to your mother if she is hesitant about your baby-sitting on a school night."

I nodded and they drove off with Tessa waving both her tiny hands. Going to the Cantrells had become a routine for me. Timmy probably would be in bed when I arrived at seven o'clock. I'd play with Tessa about an hour, then read her a story and tuck her in, and the rest of the evening I'd watch TV, or study, or read.

Two things I *couldn't* do when I was baby-sitting there were to have one of my friends over, or to talk on the phone; unless it was a necessary call and in that case it was to be kept short. Mrs. Cantrell was strict about those two rules. She told me she'd once had a sitter who was so engrossed in a personal phone conversation with the stereo going full blast at the same time that she didn't hear Tessa crying. The child was in her crib sobbing after a bad dream when the Cantrells returned.

Mr. Cantrell always came to my house for me if it was dark, and would walk me home afterwards as a safety precaution. I'd be earning money, and if I stayed home that evening I'd probably have been watching television with Mom and Dad. It suited me fine to baby-sit, since Kenny Chapman was out of town.

Five

When Fran and I were walking to school Monday morning, she wanted to know everything about my Saturday night date with Kenny. "And do I mean *everything*," she said vehemently. "Where did you go? What did you do? Did he kiss you? Start with that last question, Beth-Ann. Did he?"

"Yes, he kissed me," I said.

"A lot? Gosh, you're blushing!"

I giggled self-consciously. "I guess you could say there was a lot of kisses. I lost count of how many."

"Remember my telling you that you needed to loosen up? You must have taken my advice. Did you see him yesterday?"

I explained about Kenny's trip to Raleigh. When she asked more questions about Saturday night, I mentioned going to Vicki's. She was impressed.

"Vicki is just about the most popular girl

in the junior class," she said. "Popular with girls as well as boys. You must rate to be on her list."

"I doubt if I'm 'on her list,' whatever you mean by that."

"Oh, you know what I'm talking about. She invited you to her house."

"She didn't invite *me*. I happened to be Kenny's date, and Kenny and Whit are friends. That's why I was included."

"What does Vicki Burt have that makes everyone like her?" Fran asked in a thoughtful voice. "I've tried to analyze why popular girls are popular and can't find the answer. Vicki is pretty, but not gorgeous, and she's smart without being a real brain. She doesn't have any big talents like singing, or dancing, or gymnastics — at least, not that I know about. Yet, you never find a soul who doesn't think she's great. Why are some people liked by everybody?"

"She smiles a lot. I guess it comes down to charm — whatever charm is," I replied. "She treats everyone the same instead of being palsy-walsy with one person and an iceberg to the next, and she's naturally friendly."

I'm friendly, too. Or I try to be, I thought silently, knowing full well I didn't exude friendliness the way Vicki did. In the past embarrassment over not dating had increased my shyness, and made me withdraw into a shell. But the two dates with Kenny were already beginning to change that.

Fran and I paused at a corner to wait for a

lull in traffic so we could cross the street, and I changed the subject. "What did you and Jack do yesterday?" I asked.

"Mom told me you phoned. But when I came home it was eleven o'clock, and you know how my folks are about my talking on the phone that late. Jack and I didn't do anything spectacular. Just went to his older brother's apartment and watched an awful lot of television Sunday afternoon. Later, we picked up his brother's girl friend and the four of us ate hamburgers at McDonald's, then went back to the apartment and that TV set."

"Did Jack kiss you?" I mimicked the tone she used when she asked about Kenny and me.

"You'd better believe it! When will you see Kenny again?"

A warm sensation spread through my body. "Saturday night as he was leaving my house he said he'd see me at school today."

"You're blushing again," she announced, as if I didn't already know.

Kenny was standing outside the door of my homeroom when Fran and I reached school. After a hello to him, she promptly said she needed to go to her locker, which I thought was decent of her, since it gave Kenny and I a few minutes alone — as much alone as was possible in the hall with students everywhere.

"Hi," he grinned. "Long time no see."

Was the remark his way of letting me

know he'd missed me on Sunday, and because of it the day had seemed long to him? The idea was enchanting. I couldn't stop smiling.

"How was the birthday celebration in Raleigh?" I asked.

"Grandpa was pleased and that's what mattered. What did you do all day yesterday, Beth-Ann? Have a bunch of dates?"

His lower lip curled ever so slightly when he said "a bunch of dates," and the crazy thought hit me that he sounded as if he resented my dating someone other than him. No boy had ever spoken to me like that, and I felt ten feet tall. I even came back with a flirtatious reply, something else that was a "first," as I'd never been able to manage the sort of give-and-take conversation lots of guys and girls handled effortlessly.

"I wouldn't exactly say 'a bunch'," I began.

"How many?" He was dead serious.

"Oh, three or — " I broke the sentence off. He looked so troubled I stopped teasing. Was it possible he didn't realize I hadn't dated until two days earlier?

"If you truly want to know about my Sunday," I told him, "it wasn't the greatest. I slept most of the morning, studied in the afternoon, and baby-sat last night."

His grin returned and the stormy expression left his eyes. Before either of us could speak again, the bell rang that told us we had to go to our homerooms during the next three minutes, or be counted tardy. I was just a few feet from mine, but he had to climb two flights of stairs.

"See you at lunch," he said. "Wait for me outside the cafeteria."

When you're happy, time has a way of skipping along, and the week whizzed by. Kenny and I had a few minutes together every morning before the homeroom bell, ate lunch together, and when he finished his gym job around quarter to five, he stopped by my house on the way to his.

I was waiting each afternoon, watching for him. It seemed very right for his arms to be around me the second he was in our living room. We had only fifteen or twenty minutes alone before my parents arrived.

"Oops! Was that a car door?" One of us — usually I was the one — would say, and we sprang apart.

My mother always parked in the driveway and came in the back way, while Dad parked his car on the street in front of the house. I had a horror of their walking in to find Kenny and me kissing. It wasn't that we were doing anything wrong, because we weren't. I simply didn't want an audience, especially not my parents, even though Mom was ecstatic about my dating. I wasn't sure what Dad thought. He'd given Kenny a hard, sizing-up look when I introduced them Friday night, and he hadn't mentioned Kenny to me since.

When Mom and I tidied up the kitchen

after dinner each night, our conversation eventually got around to the subject of my dating. She'd tell me she thought Kenny was a darling, and nice. I'd agree without discussing him, because I was afraid if I talked much I would admit just how wonderful I thought he was. The tension she and I had endured for weeks before my birthday had vanished, and it was a relief for home to be peaceful once more.

My parents didn't lay down the law about no dates on school nights. They didn't need to. Kenny told me Monday afternoon he had to maintain at least a C average to keep his job with Coach Hardy.

"That means studying plenty at night," he said with a sigh. "If I flunk or get a D, I won't merely lose the job, Dad will also pocket my car keys. So, I guess I won't see you after dark until Friday."

"It doesn't seem fair to base your job on grades," I protested.

"I'm being paid with school funds, and Coach is a stickler about grades. There are a dozen guys waiting for my job if I goof off."

When I was silent because I didn't know what to say, he added, "If I don't have a job, I won't have cash to put gas in the car, or to have fun on weekends, Beth-Ann." He squeezed my hand, his fingers warm on mine. "We'll have our quota of dates this weekend. Okay with you?"

"You know it is."

It was hard for me to concentrate on studying because I thought about Kenny all the time, storing up tidbits of information in my mind about things he liked and disliked. Sometimes, with an open textbook in front of my eyes, instead of doing lessons I'd mull over what I knew about him: remembering that he hated the color purple, and thought yellow shirts were fabulous, and that pizza was his favorite food, with chocolate pie a close second. He'd told me he enjoyed police shows on TV, especially the ones with car chase scenes. He loathed everything connected with history, and hoped someday to have a pilot's license, and his own airplane.

On Thursday an extension phone was installed in my room, and I called Fran about 8 p.m. when I was supposed to be writing a theme for English. I was dying to call Kenny, but didn't have the nerve to phone his house for fear his mother or father would answer. I might be getting over my shyness, but I wasn't at ease telephoning a boy, particularly if it meant talking to his parents.

"Your own phone — lucky you," Fran said. "I wish that day would come for me. I can't talk long tonight, though. I have to cram for two tests tomorrow. Anyway, if I'm on the phone too long Dad will start to look at his watch."

"I ought to be studying," I admitted. "But I'm not in the mood."

"I'll bet you're in the mood to think about Kenny."

"Something like that." I laughed softly.

"My outlook certainly is different now that he's a part of my life."

"Your status at school has improved, too, Beth-Ann."

"What do you mean?"

"Several girls have asked me about you and Kenny."

I gave a gasp. "Asked you what?"

"Oh, how long you've been dating him, and how serious you two are, and — "

The phone clicked twice, which meant the receiver had been picked up and put down in her house or mine. Instantly, Mom was at my door.

"Getting the extension phone doesn't mean you're to monopolize the line," she snapped. "Your father would like to make a business call. Have you done all your homework?"

I mumbled a sheepish no. Fran and I hung up immediately.

Apparently it wasn't only the girls at school who were aware of my dating. A couple of guys I scarcely knew went out of their way to speak to me between classes, something that hadn't happened before. One was Chris Abernathy, the boy I'd seen Sunday afternoon in the convenience store. He caught up with me in the hall after English one day.

"How's the world treating you, Beth-Ann?" he asked.

"Fine." I tried to cover my surprise. "What about you?"

He made the okay sign with his thumb and forefinger. With his dark red hair and winsome smile, Chris was cute, although not as handsome as Kenny in my estimation.

I had taken for granted that dating would be fun, but I hadn't expected it to open a shining, new world. Being seen with a boy apparently put me in a different category from the lackluster Beth-Ann Hughes I used to be. Nothing about it made sense, because I was still basically the same as always, though I didn't feel colorless or unwanted any longer. I was so happy I glowed.

One small disappointment marred the week and I tried to overlook it. Each afternoon when Kenny dropped by my house I hoped he might suggest our going steady. When he didn't, I rationalized that it wasn't necessary for him to ask the question or for me to answer since the other indications were right. He couldn't be dating anyone else, since his spare time was spent with me, and I certainly wasn't going with another boy. At school, he often held my hand, and our afternoon kisses were pure heaven. Seeing one another exclusively was the same as going steady despite our not making a verbal commitment, wasn't it?

The weekend didn't turn out as I anticipated, although being with Kenny was what counted.

Maybe I'm hooked on his kisses, I thought and smiled at my reflection in the mirror Friday morning while I dressed for school. My lips looked soft, and there was a fresh

59

sparkle in my eyes. When you've ached to be noticed or wanted by a boy and have almost given up hope and then it happens — it's like living under the arc of a rainbow.

Reality set in at noon Friday when Kenny turned to me and said, "I won't be any later tonight than I can help, Beth-Ann. Wait for me in the gym after the game."

We were sitting side by side in the cafeteria, with five minutes of the lunch hour remaining. The others at our table had finished eating and were straggling out, everyone talking about the basketball game scheduled for that evening. Since Kenny loved sports, I had assumed we'd attend the game. I'd also assumed he and I would sit together, and wondered what his statement about not being late implied.

"*After* the game?" I asked, my voice raspy. A lump as big as a hard-boiled egg jumped into my throat.

He gave me a quizzical look. "You know I have to work during all the games, don't you, Beth-Ann?"

I shook my head. I hadn't gone to any night sports events in the past. All week I'd been counting the hours until Friday, and it was a blow that Kenny had to work.

"With my job, I go to all games for whatever sport is in season," he explained. "It's not a bad deal, to be paid to watch something I'd watch anyway."

I gnawed my lower lip, deliberately staring straight ahead rather than at him.

"The thing for you to do is to get a ride to school tonight," he went on. "You won't be waiting by yourself when the game ends because the team members have their girl friends wait in the gym, too."

"I'd rather come to school when you come, Kenny."

"You can't. I probably won't go home after classes today. The team doesn't practice on game days, but Coach Hardy has a strategy session, and has food sent in for all of us at four-thirty. After the game I have to hang around in the locker room with Biff Collier, the team manager, until everyone is finished in the showers. We won't clean up or wash towels or uniforms tonight; that can be taken care of in the morning."

He would work Saturday morning, too. The lump in my throat was growing.

"What's wrong, Beth-Ann?" he asked. "Are you mad about something? You look mad."

"Of course not." It was a fib. I was disappointed, and angry that he hadn't mentioned his schedule earlier. "I — uh — was thinking — about a ride to the gym. I don't want to tag along on someone else's date."

"Good gosh! You won't be tagging along! Just ask anybody."

The bell saved me from replying. I don't know what I'd have said if it had been necessary for me to speak.

At the close of school I hurried to Fran's locker to ask if I could ride with her and Jack, seeing an odd twist to her mouth when I phrased the question.

"You could if we were going to the game," she said.

"Oh?"

She buttoned her coat as she explained. "Our team has such a rotten record for the year that Jack says he can't take another defeat. I guess we'll bowl instead."

Couldn't you and Jack take me to the game on your way to the bowling alley? I thought without asking aloud. Mom or Dad would drive me if I requested it, but everyone at school made fun of students who were chauffeured by their parents now that we were juniors and had reached our middle teens. Too, there was the grim chance that my father might decide he'd like to come in and see the basketball game, and that would be humiliating since other parents didn't chaperone their kids.

"Beth-Ann, there's Vicki Burt," Fran said. "Ask her."

"Ask me what?" Vicki inquired, pausing by Fran and me.

Her smile was warm as I explained about Kenny working and made my request. "Sure," she answered. "Chris and I would love to give you a ride. I have a date with Chris Abernathy tonight. The game's at eight, and he's going to come for me at half past seven. We'll stop for you a few minutes later."

She acted as if she was genuinely glad for me to tag along, and my spirits lifted. I knew at least one reason why Vicki was so well liked.

At the game Friday night I didn't feel much a part of what was going on. I seemed to be looking at the game, and at the people in the gym as though I was gazing at a movie screen, watching the action but removed from it. Vicki insisted on my sitting with her and Chris and I did, but I still felt alone.

The noise was terrific — voices reverberated and feet stomped constantly. The cheerleaders shouted, and students joined in the school yells. I smelled popcorn and chocolate candy bars, their odors almost sickening as the air in the gym grew unbearably hot. Occasionally, I had glimpses of Kenny. Once he went out and returned with a clipboard that he gave to an assistant coach, and another time he ran to the edge of the basketball court, visibly upset when an official penalized one of our players. Although from where I sat, most of the time he was hidden from my view.

The score was close, 48–46, but we lost. The crowd from the other school, sitting across the gym, erupted loudly when it was over. Students on our side were quiet as they filed out.

"Want Chris and me to wait with you until Kenny comes?" Vicki asked.

I would have liked that but shook my head, assuring her I was okay. Other girls were waiting as Kenny had said they would.

But I was the last one left, sitting alone in the bleachers when Kenny finally came out of the locker room with Biff Collier, who must not have had a date. By then there was a throbbing pain in the bottom of my stomach because I was terrified that Kenny had forgotten me. He hadn't brought me to a game before, and maybe he wasn't accustomed to dating on game nights. Correction, I thought darkly, he hadn't brought me at all; he'd asked me to meet him there.

When he came toward me he grinned and my heart melted. "Did you think I was standing you up?" he asked, and winked at the same moment.

"I hoped you weren't." Returning his smile was a reflex action, my gloom gone.

"It'll never happen, Beth-Ann. Let's go some place and grab a burger. I'm starved."

I was hungry for time alone with Kenny, not food, though I didn't tell him that.

Six

February became March and I settled easily into the dating routine, aware of how great it was to have a boyfriend. Sometimes, though, when I was in a completely honest mood, I admitted to myself that Kenny could be a tiny bit boring.

To myself. The phrase was important. Nobody else knew how I felt, and I'd have choked to death before mentioning it. After months of sitting home dateless, being with a guy was wonderful.

Still, it bothered me that Kenny and I didn't talk about any subjects except school, his job, or sports. His idea of a good time on a weekend date was for us to wander around a shopping center for hours. I didn't expect or want him to spend a lot of money on entertainment, but there were museums, and exhibits we could have attended without cost. Or we could have teamed up with another couple to play Trivial Pursuit, or some other game, or just to gab. If we happened to bump into kids we knew at the shopping centers and went for Cokes in a group, it was fine with him. But he absolutely refused to line up a double date in advance or plan something different, and that attitude led to our first quarrel.

Maybe "quarrel" is too strong a word, since we didn't bombard one another with ugly comebacks, or make cutting remarks. It was our first disagreement, though, and the first time I'd questioned what we did on dates. It hurt for him to ignore my wishes, as if he thought I was too dumb to have good ideas.

I knew every potted plant at the malls in our area of Richmond, every window display, where every store was located. Meandering from one bench to another had grown tiresome since we'd done it so much — something I mentioned to him on a March Friday night as we were getting into his car at my house. The weather was cold, and Kenny had just expressed thankfulness that the shopping center was enclosed and heated.

"Not a shopping center again," I muttered under my breath, and he overheard me. I hadn't meant to speak aloud, but I was thinking it and the words just came from my mouth.

The look he gave me could only be described as exasperated. "Just what do you suggest, Beth-Ann?" he asked roughly. "It's no fun hanging around your house with your parents staring at us."

He didn't need to remind me. There was no way to have privacy in my house, and that was it.

Glancing at Kenny as he put the key into the ignition, I said, "Why don't we see if Fran and Jack would like to make it a foursome for tonight? Fran has Trivial Pursuit and — "

He didn't let me finish. "I wouldn't miss Jack Dayton if the pavement opened up and sucked him in right before my eyes, Beth-Ann!"

I gasped, speechless for a second. "What an awful thing to say," I blurted out finally.

"I know Fran Simmons is a good friend of yours, but I'm not going to pal around with a jerk like Jack. He's always making lousy cracks about our basketball team, and about our having had a losing season." A growling noise came from deep inside Kenny's throat. "Sure, we've lost more games than we've won this year, but that's no reason for him to be so darn negative all the time."

He pulled the car away from the curb. Gnawing my lower lip, I tried again. "What about Whit and Vicki? We could — "

"Whit's home with an ear infection, and I don't know what Vicki is doing tonight. Good grief, Beth-Ann! What's wrong with our date being just you and me? Do I have bubonic plague or something?"

"Of course not." I made myself smile, hoping he noticed, and touched his arm, sliding my fingers down to cover his hand on the steering wheel.

We were silent for several minutes, my hands in my lap once more. I wondered about our date at the pizza restaurant back in February when we joined Whit and Vicki, deciding the two boys hadn't planned in advance to meet there as I'd first thought. Kenny was possessive and he could be anti-social at times. As I glanced at his profile while we were in the car that March night, I decided this was one of *those* evenings.

Kenny appeared to be concentrating on his driving. When he had to stop for a red traffic light, I drew a long breath and changed the subject, mentioning the history assignment Mrs. Holmes had given our class for the weekend. It was a mistake on my part. Kenny snorted; he disliked history and I knew it. Any other topic would have been better.

He found a parking place at the mall and I knew we'd do the same old thing: walk around and swap greetings with any students we recognized. Saturday night would be similar, unless Kenny decided he'd like to go to the movies. The bright spot would come when he drove me home and we kissed good-night in the parked car. There would be additional kisses when he came in with me. My parents would be in their room by then.

* * *

The second quarrel — a big one — came a week later on a Saturday afternoon. Richmond was having a taste of spring with warm sunshine and a bright blue sky. The temperature was more like May than March, and it was a lovely change from winter. Forsythia bushes in the yards on my street were in bloom, their vivid golden flowers cascading gracefully down the long branches. Tree buds had begun to swell and clumps of crocus, the first of the bulb flowers, made dabs of rich purple colors on the ground by our front door.

Kenny arrived shortly after lunch that Saturday, and when I met him in the driveway, we looked at each other and laughed. We were dressed identically, both of us wearing blue jeans and yellow knit shirts. I'd deliberately chosen my shirt because I knew he liked yellow.

"We're a matched pair," I said and giggled. "Isn't it a gorgeous day? Let's do something outdoors."

"What do you have in mind, Beth-Ann?"

"Do you really want to know?"

He nodded, and I said, "I'd like to ride over to Williamsburg."

Kenny's smile disappeared and his shoulders stiffened. Williamsburg, the eighteenth century village that once was the capital of Virginia, had restored government buildings furnished with antiques and quaint, postage-stamp-sized houses, some of them still occupied by descendants of the early settlers. Those homes weren't open to the public, but they were set close to the streets, and tiny gardens were visible through white picket fences.

Cars weren't permitted in this historical area, so Kenny and I would have to park. But we could stroll about, and it was fun to watch the people who worked there because they wore colonial outfits, the men in knee britches and three-cornered hats, the women in long dresses with shawls or capes instead of coats. Williamsburg was only sixty miles from Richmond, an easy distance for an afternoon outing. I'd been there many times and realized Kenny must have, too, but I always found something interesting to see.

The expression on his face made me attempt to qualify my suggestion. He looked disgusted at the mention of Williamsburg.

"I don't mean we'd go into any of the buildings or take a sightseeing tour," I added quickly. "We can walk down Duke of Gloucester Street, though, and see the shops and maybe get a couple of gingerbread men from the bakery. I never get tired of watching the tourists."

"No way!" he barked. "I despise that colonial junk!"

I recoiled at the force of his answer; it was almost as if he'd slapped me. Maybe I should have kept quiet after his outburst, but I didn't. His refusal was disappointing, and I was irked by his attitude.

"You really shouldn't be so anti-history," I said.

That made him even more angry. He glared at me fiercely. "Are you telling me what to like and dislike?" he retorted.

"No, but we live in the section of Virginia where the first permanent settlement in this country was made and people come from all over the world to visit Jamestown and Williamsburg. It's not vital for you and I to go there today if you object, but you shouldn't be so negative about history."

"Negative? Me? You're a fine one to talk about being negative! Just shut up about it! Okay?"

"Don't speak to me like that, Kenny Chapman!"

"I'll speak any way I please! Let's get one thing straight, Beth-Ann. I happen to be living in the twentieth century and I'm glad of it. I like space flights and computers and TV and a bunch of other modern stuff, and it bores me to death to talk about history!"

"I like modern things, too." My voice was hoarse with tension, although I made an effort to sound calm. "But that doesn't mean I don't appreciate the past."

"There you go again!" he hissed. "Talk about a one-track mind — you've got it! Haven't you heard a word I just said? Why don't you dry up and get off your soap box?"

That was too much. I looked squarely into his face. "Another thing I don't want is for us to stand here and argue in my front yard," I said through clenched jaws. "Lately nothing I say or do suits you, and any suggestions I make seem to rub you the wrong way, Kenny. If we're going to fight, for heaven's sake let's go in the house where the neighbors won't hear us."

"I'm getting out of here on the double! You don't need to worry about your neighbors hearing me, or seeing me, or anything else, because I won't annoy you anymore! That's a promise!"

Brushing past me, he took long steps to reach his car, quickly slamming the door hard as he slid under the steering wheel. He had the motor racing before I could reply, and he was out of sight around the corner instantly.

I wanted to cry, and couldn't because it took all my strength to breathe, and I was panting as if I'd been running. The air, balmy though it was, scalded my lungs. In the past I hadn't disagreed with Kenny and it was hard to believe he'd be livid over something so unimportant like my suggestion that we go to Williamsburg.

Maybe another matter is bothering him, I thought, attempting to rationalize. He'll be back soon, I know he will. He'll cool off and his conscience will hurt, and he'll either return, or phone. . . .

Moving deliberately, I went into the living room. The house was strangely quiet as I sat down on the sofa, my ice cold hands clumped into fists. Before Kenny came, Mom and Dad had left to take care of some errands. Now I was relieved that they'd gone, because if they were at home they might have overheard the argument. Even if that didn't happen, my mother would have taken one look at my face and known something was wrong. I wasn't ready to discuss Kenny's and my quarrel.

He'll be back soon, I repeated silently. I know he will.

The afternoon dragged on. The telephone didn't ring. Twice when I heard cars on the street, I ran to the front window, but neither of those cars belonged to Kenny. My back felt as stiff as Kenny's looked when I mentioned Williamsburg; my shoulders were hunched forward. Every nerve in my body was taut.

It was nearly four o'clock when my parents came in. Mom had a bag of groceries and Dad was carrying a suit he'd picked up at the cleaners. I heard their voices before they opened the front door, their words to each other laced with laughter.

Mom's eyebrows lifted in surprise when she saw me. "Where's Kenny?" she asked. "I thought you were going out with him."

"He — uh — he was here, but — he had to — to go," I stammered.

She wasn't fooled. "Is anything wrong, Beth-Ann?"

"Wrong? I don't know what you mean."

It was a lie, of course.

"Anything wrong between you and Kenny?" she persisted. "You look as if you've lost your last friend."

"Everything is fine. It's — " Looking at her was my undoing and my voice broke when I met her eyes. "No, it's not fine," I choked the words out. "Kenny and I had an argument and — and he left in a huff. He's mad because I wanted to go to Williamsburg this afternoon, and he hates everything connected with history."

She sat beside me on the sofa. Dad had carried his suit to their bedroom, and I could hear him moving about in that part of the house.

"Were you trying to force Kenny to go some place he didn't want to go?" Mom said.

"No. I mentioned it and he got angry as soon as I mentioned Williamsburg."

"Really, Beth-Ann! Was your going there important enough for you two to have an argument?" She seemed to be criticizing me. "It doesn't appear to be worth a quarrel. Why didn't you talk about it first and — "

"We couldn't discuss it!" I cut in. "He lost his temper and — Oh, Mom — "

I burst into tears, covering my face with my hands, sobs shaking my shoulders. She put her arm around me and rubbed her hand up and down my back, not speaking, letting me cry for a few minutes.

"I — I'm sorry," I managed when the sobs stopped, and the whole story tumbled out. I told her everything that happened during the afternoon, repeating what I'd said as well as Kenny's ugly remarks. I thought she'd side with me, but she looked doubtful.

"Boys don't like bossy girls," she commented.

"Mom, I don't think I was bossy. I merely

made a suggestion, and — " I swallowed hard. "Girls don't like bossy boys, either. It should be a fifty-fifty thing, or at least people should be able to discuss things."

"Kenny seems like a very nice boy, Beth-Ann. Don't you want to continue dating him?"

The question startled me. I hadn't considered *not* wanting it. My anger was all mixed up with hurt and at the moment, hurt seemed to be the stronger emotion. It was a shock for her not to be more understanding.

"Yes, in a way I guess I do," I admitted, shivering at the prospect of being dateless once more, even though I didn't think I could endure another bitter scene with Kenny.

"If you started the quarrel, Beth-Ann, shouldn't you be the one to apologize to him?"

"But I didn't start it! You assume I'm guilty, and I'm not!"

She didn't answer and her eyes bored into me. I'd have given anything to know what she was thinking.

"I guess I argued as much as he did. But he got angry first, and I didn't make the terrible remarks to him that he made to me." I sighed. "I'll apologize if he gives me half a chance, if he apologizes, too, but I don't think I'll grovel."

After a short silence she left me alone. A million disjointed thoughts raced through my head. I wanted Kenny to come to me, so we could straighten everything out and date again. Yet I didn't want trouble between us and knew instinctively we'd fight again unless I gave in to his every whim. When we first began to date I was so overwhelmed by having a boy want to be with me that I'd let him call all the shots. Now, I felt I should have a say-so in what we did, and where we went. Was that so wrong? I asked myself that question and wasn't sure of the answer.

Maybe Mom was correct, and I'd become bossy, though I couldn't believe making a suggestion about what we'd do on a specific afternoon was bossy. If Kenny had said, Let's not go to Williamsburg, or, I'd rather do something else, I wouldn't have insisted. But he'd been so nasty. I didn't like to think our future weekends would be spent in first one shopping mall, then in another. I wasn't sure what I wanted to do, except that I longed to feel happy once more. Instead, I was miserable.

Five o'clock came, then six. There was no message from Kenny, nor any sign of him. When my mother began supper preparations, I shuddered at the idea of food. We usually had hamburgers and baked beans on Saturday night and the thought of eating made my stomach churn.

I decided Kenny must have meant what he'd said about not "annoying" me anymore. But his kisses certainly weren't annoying, far from it. Just thinking about those kisses made my lips burn. If he had walked into our house at that minute, I'd have gone into his arms.

76

But he didn't walk in, and a strange question began to nag me. Did I enjoy kissing Kenny Chapman? Or did I merely like to kiss and be kissed? So that kissing another boy, if I cared about him at all, would have given me an equal amount of pleasure?

I'd daydreamed about Kenny for so long before our first date that I'd expected his kisses to be heavenly, and they were. Still, he was the only boy I'd ever dated or kissed. And on that March Saturday, weeks after the rainy afternoon he gave me a ride home from school, his stinging remarks about our going to Williamsburg were a searing memory. I wasn't really sure how I felt about him.

Mom insisted on my coming to the supper table, and we'd just taken our seats when the telephone rang. Dad started to get up to answer, but I bounded from my chair and ran into my room to have privacy, plopping down on the foot of my bed.

It wasn't Kenny, it was Mrs. Cantrell on the line.

"Beth-Ann, is it possible for you to baby-sit tonight?" she asked. "Richard and I are invited to his boss's home for dinner. Mrs. Hollingsworth was going to stay with the children, but she called me ten minutes ago to say she's fallen, and thinks her ankle might be broken. Her son is on his way to her house to take her to the hospital for X-rays."

"That's a shame," I said. Mrs. Hollingsworth was a widow who lived farther down the street.

"If you can't make it tonight," Mrs. Cantrell went on, "do you know anybody reliable we can get on short notice? I'd cancel our plans and stay home if this wasn't an evening with Richard's boss, but I feel we ought to go, if possible."

I had to make an instant decision. Kenny wasn't going to contact me that night, I was positive of it. And even if he did, after ignoring me for hours, I didn't want to be sitting at home waiting. Maybe that was a perverse attitude on my part, but I had too much pride to let him think I'd be his puppet.

"Yes, Mrs. Cantrell," I said. "I'll be glad to stay with Tessa and Timmy."

"You're a lifesaver, Beth-Ann. Can you be ready in half an hour?"

I assured her I would, and eased the phone into its cradle, and sat very still on the edge of the bed before doing an odd thing. Jumping up, I pulled the yellow knit shirt — Kenny's favorite color — over my head. Scrambling in my chest of drawers, I took out a blue sweater. I didn't want to wear any garment that would remind me of Kenny Chapman until my thoughts were sorted out, and my emotions were back to normal.

Returning to the supper table, I discovered as I picked up the hamburger that it was possible to swallow a small bite.

"I told Mrs. Cantrell I'd baby-sit this evening," I said to my parents, glancing first

78

at Mom and then at Dad. "If Kenny comes over or phones, just say I've gone out. Don't tell him where I am or what I'm doing."

Both of them nodded, and to my surprise, Dad said, "Don't worry about this afternoon any more than you can help, Beth-Ann."

Mom must have told him about the fight. "I can't help worrying," I murmured.

"Honey, dating and breaking up are all part of growing up," he went on. "You'll go out with a lot of boys before you settle on one for keeps in the future — way off in the future. And that's how it should be. If you and Kenny patch things up between you, and it's what the two of you want, good enough. But if this split is permanent, don't feel it's the end of the world for either of you. The sun will keep right on rising in the east every morning, and another boy will be in the picture for you before long."

I doubted that bit about "another boy," though I didn't say so. It gave my morale a boost for Dad to understand, especially since my mother seemed to feel Kenny had been right and I was wrong.

Later I thought back over the events of that March Saturday, and I wondered how I would have reacted at supper if I'd known that going to the Cantrells to baby-sit on short notice was about to change my life.

Seven

"Timmy is already asleep, and I want Tessa in bed no later than eight o'clock, if she can hold her eyes open that long," Mrs. Cantrell said as she handed me a slip of paper with the phone number where she and her husband could be reached in case of an emergency. "The weather was so beautiful today that both children played outside all afternoon and they're tired. Tessa," — she turned to the child, who looked adorable in bright red pajamas — "go find a book so Beth-Ann can read you a story."

As the little girl trotted off, her mother spoke to me in an undertone. "There's a lemon layer cake in the kitchen, and Cokes and sandwich meat in the refrigerator, so help yourself." She added, "But please wait to eat until Tessa is asleep. She had a big slice of cake after supper, and that's enough sweets for now."

Tessa and I stood at the living room window and waved as her parents drove away. I had to suppress a chuckle when I saw the book the child selected. It was her favorite, one I'd read to her many times. She knew it by heart, although she always wanted the same fairy stories and poems over and over again. If I left out a single word, she'd correct me.

We settled down in a big wing chair, Tessa snuggled against my side. While I read, she pointed to pictures in the book, turning pages at the proper times. After a little while she yawned and became so still, I realized she was sleepy, and sneaked a look at my watch. It was ten minutes to eight.

"That's the end of the story," I said, as if she didn't know. "Let's go upstairs now."

"Just one more story, Beth-Ann. Please."

"Ill tell you what we'll do. We'll go to your room and after you're in bed I'll read you a poem. How about that?"

"Two poems?"

"All right, two poems," I answered, and laughed softly. Tessa drove a hard bargain.

The child fitted her small hand into mine as we crossed the living room to the stairs. We were on the fourth step when the doorbell rang. The sound startled me in the quiet house. It might be more accurate to say it frightened me, because if Mrs. Cantrell had been expecting anyone, she'd have mentioned it. Night had fallen outside and all of a sudden I was aware of being alone with the responsibility of two young children.

I pushed Tessa down on the fourth step. "Sit there while I see who's at the door," I told her, trying to ignore the way my heart was thumping.

I wasn't about to open the door instantly. Going to the front window, I peeped around the drapes, hoping I wouldn't be seen. The outside light was burning and a man was on the stoop. His face was averted and I couldn't make out his features, but he was tall with brown hair. He wore a pale tan windbreaker, and faded blue jeans with dirt smears on the pants legs. He moved slightly while I was watching, and I saw his profile with a dark smudge of dirt on his cheek. Nothing about him was familiar. I was sure I'd never seen him before.

The bell rang again.

"Beth-Ann, who is it?" Tessa asked. "Why don't you open the door?" She remained on the fourth step, but she'd risen to her feet.

"Shhhh. Sit down and don't talk." I held my finger to my lips as a signal for her to be quiet.

"Is this a game, Beth-Ann?"

"Yes. A game." I forced a smile to reassure her, though she seemed more curious than scared. I was the scared one.

If I didn't speak or open the door, I reasoned, the man would think nobody was home and go away. Then I realized I was being dumb to hope he would leave. If he was a burglar and believed the house was empty, he would break in.

The bell rang once more, a long ring that time with the man holding his finger on the button. The chimes echoed through the house.

"If you don't know how to open the door, Beth-Ann, I'll show you," Tessa said, and started down the stairs.

At that instant the man yelled, "Is anybody home?"

I couldn't continue to stand in one spot. I had to act before Tessa reached the door. The child's eyes were on me as she came down another step.

"Can I do something for you?" I called through the closed door, peeping around the drapes again, and motioning for Tessa to stay behind me.

"Margaret?" the man yelled. Margaret was Mrs. Cantrell's first name. "This is the Cantrell house, isn't it?" the stranger asked, and stepped backward to check the house number. I saw his face then, and except for the dirt, he was decent looking, even handsome. He didn't appear to be much older than I was. I guessed his age at seventeen or eighteen.

"Who's in there?" he asked.. "Open up! Where are Margaret and Richard Cantrell?"

I was still apprehensive and not about to let a stranger in, even though he seemed to know the Cantrells. That might be a ruse. I'd read a lot of articles on the ways thieves and con men operated. He could be a pervert who had obtained Mr. and Mrs. Cantrell's first names from the city directory. Or a person with a grudge against one of them, or a rapist. I shuddered, trying not to think about the possibilities.

"I'm the baby-sitter," I said, fighting to hold my voice steady. "If you have a message for the Cantrells, give it to me and I'll notify them."

"I'm Tony Roberts, Margaret Cantrell's brother," he called through the door. "It's okay to open up. I'm family."

"Tony! Tony!" Tessa raced for the door. "Beth-Ann, it's Tony! He wants to come in!"

She reached the knob, but before she could turn it I snatched her hand back. The man must have guessed what was happening in the living room because he said, "I don't blame you for being cautious, but I really am Margaret's brother. Look on top of the bookcase by the door to the dining room and you'll see a bunch of framed photographs. One is an enlarged snapshot of Margaret's family, and I'm the guy on the extreme left wearing a red sweater. Gosh, I hope Margaret hasn't rearranged the furniture since the last time I was in Richmond. After you take a look at it, open the door with the chain bolt hooked and see if I'm not the person in that snapshot. Surely you don't believe Margaret would have the picture of a hardcore criminal in her living room, do you?"

I did as he asked. The snapshot was where he'd said it would be, and when I cracked the door with the chain bolt in place to compare the man with the picture, Tessa jumped up and down again, squealing, "Tony! It's Tony!" I unhooked the chain and she hurled herself at him.

"Man, you're growing!" he told her as he picked her up in his arms. "I like those red pj's. How about letting me wear them?"

"Tony, you're too big." She giggled.

He set her down and looked at me. "I guess I scared you," he grinned. "You're too smart not to give a big welcome to somebody you don't know, but I really am Margaret's brother."

"I'm Beth-Ann Hughes, the baby-sitter," I answered. "The Cantrells are at a dinner party, and will be back between eleven and midnight."

"Tony, your face is dirty. Your pants are, too." Tessa giggled again.

"Yep, you're right," he said. "That's the reason I'm here. To take a shower. To see you and your mommy and dad, too."

"And Timmy. Don't you want to see Timmy?"

"Sure. I wouldn't leave him out."

"Tony, how did your face get dirty?" she asked.

I'd wondered the same thing. He grinned again, showing very white teeth. He had the bluest eyes I'd ever seen.

"I've spent the entire day on an archaeological dig and that means being down on my knees, Tessa. In the dirt, no less. I'd planned to drive home tonight but if the good weather holds, the dig will continue tomorrow. So I figured Margaret and Richard would let me have a bed tonight, and a shower. I need that shower right away."

I was immediately interested. "An archaeological dig? Where? Near Richmond?"

"Just east of Williamsburg. I was there last fall, helping with a similar dig, and everything stopped when the cold weather came. But now, an apartment complex is going to be built near the James River. When the real estate developers brought in bulldozers, they unearthed some signs of former inhabitants on the site — the partial foundation of a house and some pottery shards. So, the big excavating equipment was put on hold, and the archaeologists were given thirty days to see what they can find in the ground in the way of historical relics."

I listened, fascinated, but Tessa didn't pay attention to what he was saying. She pulled at his hand. "Are you going to play ball with me, Tony?" she asked.

"You bet, but not tonight. You're already in your pj's. Doesn't that mean you're ready for bed? Besides, I'd get you dirty since I'm so dirty and you wouldn't want that."

"Oops, Tessa, it's past your bedtime," I told her. "Your mother said you were to be tucked in by eight, it's half an hour past that. So let's go upstairs."

"But I want to stay up and see Tony, Beth-Ann."

"I'll be here for breakfast and we'll play

then. But right now I'm going to my car to get some clean clothes, then I'm going to take a shower. Promise you'll be fast asleep by the time I finish. Okay?"

She nodded solemnly and looked at me. "Will you still read me two poems?" she asked, and yawned again.

I told her I would, but she was asleep before I finished the second one, her breathing deep and regular. I adjusted the night light and tiptoed out, glancing at my reflection as I passed the mirror on her bureau. My eyes had a sparkle that wasn't there when I left home, and I felt a familiar excitement.

The shower was still running when I went downstairs. I found a magazine and looked at the pictures, unable to concentrate on reading, more concerned with the nearness of Tony Roberts. I hadn't even known Mrs. Cantrell had a brother, much less such a handsome one. The Cantrells had moved into the house across the street from us a year earlier, and I hadn't seen much of them except when I was baby-sitting.

Tony looked scrubbed as he ran down the steps. He had on a fresh pair of jeans, and a plaid sports shirt, droplets of shower water still clinging to his hair.

"That was a million-dollar bath," he said, and grinned at me. "Margaret usually has food in the house and I think I'll forage. The two hot dogs that were my supper didn't fill me up."

Mentioning the lemon cake and sandwich

meat, I followed him into the kitchen. I cut each of us a slice of cake and watched while he made himself a mammoth sandwich.

"Tell me about the dig," I said. "It sounds wonderful."

"I enjoy it. Lots of people don't, I guess, because it's work, but it's good work. That is, if you don't mind getting dirty, and can put up with doing it all day without any results."

"You mean you didn't find anything today?"

"An Indian arrowhead and half a brick. The brick appeared to be handmade, though, and the guy in charge of the dig seemed to think it was important. Several of the others found pottery shards, and one girl dug up the neck of a hand-blown bottle."

"I hate to show my ignorance, Tony, but what's a shard?"

"A fragment of pottery. Back in the early days people didn't have any way of getting rid of broken stuff that wouldn't burn, so usually they put things like broken dishes in an abandoned well or just dug a pit. Or they left them lying on the ground and let soil gradually cover them. Some of the shards are tiny, but some are big enough to be fitted together like pieces of a puzzle, until you almost end up with a whole plate or bowl. It shows you the kind of dishes they used." He looked at me and cocked his eyes toward his sandwich with an inch-thick filling of meat, cheese, and lettuce. "Think I can stretch my mouth to bite that?" he asked.

"Give it a go," I said.

He took a huge bite and then a long sip of Coke. "You're an amazing girl, Beth-Ann," he said. "Most people think going to a dig is a waste of time."

"I love everything about history. How did you get included in the dig?"

"I was lucky. My history teacher is a good friend of the archaeologist who is in charge. Mr. Hawkins, my teacher, brought me down last fall because he knew how much I wanted to come. I made the trip with him a couple of weekends, and we pitched a tent at the site and camped. It's not a paying job for him, or me, either. The trained archaeologists are on salary, but the rest of us are volunteers. Any items we find go to the historical foundation for safekeeping and possible exhibition later. I enjoy doing it and got a real thrill last week when Mr. Hawkins asked if I'd like to come this weekend. He had a bit of bad luck at the last minute, though. He cut his foot badly and couldn't make it, so I came alone."

"I'm full of questions. But I want to know how you start when you're ready to dig."

"Very carefully. First we outline the area with string. Then it's laid off in grids of about three feet square. Each of us digging is assigned a plot. That gives us boundaries, plus it lets a record be kept of where items are found. The plot looks tiny when you begin, but it's a big chore once you're trying to sift through it."

"Did you take your own shovel?"

"Shovel?" He threw back his head and laughed. "No way. A shovel is a no-no because it's too heavy, and might break whatever is found. You dig with a kitchen spoon, or a garden trowel, or your hands. Real carefully, too. When you come across something you dust the dirt off with a paint brush, and wash it off, then take it to one of the trained people for inspection — that is, if it's solid like a metal object or a shard. You don't move a bone."

"You found human bones?"

"Not at this site, but some diggers have. One of the guys digging next to me found a bunch of fish bones at another site. The acidity of the soil apparently preserved them, and it tells you what the early settlers and the Indians ate."

He had no way of knowing how envious I was, but I didn't say anything about it. After another bite of his sandwich, he murmured, "Mmmmm. Good."

I wanted to hear more about the dig, but I also wanted to know about him. "Where are you from?" I asked.

"Northern Virginia, Falls Church, not far from Washington, D.C." He laid his sandwich on a paper towel and grinned at me. "Know what? You're finding out a lot about me, Beth-Ann, and I don't know a darn thing about you. Have you lived in Richmond all your life?"

"Not quite all, but I don't remember living anywhere else. What about you?"

"Falls Church from the day I was born. Do you go to school in Richmond?"

Nodding, I mentioned the name of my high school. "I'm a junior. What about you, Tony?"

"A senior, and right now I'm sweating it out, waiting for a college acceptance. I have applications in at several schools, and they're supposed to let me know something before the first of May at the latest."

"Are you planning to major in history or archaeology?"

I was amazed at how many questions I was asking. It was easy to talk to Tony. My old shyness at being with a boy seemed to have disappeared, now that we were discussing a topic of interest to both of us.

"Nope. I'm opting for law," he replied. "Of course, I might change my mind. History and archaeology will always be my hobbies, though."

"I have another year of high school, which keeps me from having to decide on a college or a career for a while."

He had finished the sandwich and was eating his cake when his eyes met mine. "What do you do for fun when you aren't studying or baby-sitting?" he asked.

The question caught me by surprise. There was no reason for me to blush, but heat flowed into my face and it had to be fiery red. "Oh, I watch TV, talk with friends, go to the movies — that sort of stuff," I said.

"No dating?"

"Sure, I date." My cheeks felt rosy again, and I wondered if I should have used past tense about dating after the fuss with Kenny, although I didn't qualify my answer. "What about you, Tony?"

"I play a lot of tennis, and like to read. The last two summers I've worked as a lifeguard. And there's the dig."

He didn't say whether or not he dated, and I didn't have the nerve to ask him a direct question about it. He finished his cake — I'd eaten mine while he was on the sandwich. After I washed our plates and glasses, we returned to the living room to talk chiefly about the dig and our schools, never getting back to personal topics. I was furious with myself for not finding out if he had a special girl. I probably could have inquired since he'd mentioned dating, but the time to phrase the question passed, and I would have felt awkward tossing it at him out of the blue.

The Cantrells' return meant the end of a marvelous evening for me. They gave Tony an excited welcome, and after Mr. Cantrell paid me, he said, "Come on, Beth-Ann, I'll walk you home."

"Richard, I'll do that," Tony said instantly.

My heartbeat quickened. I had been wondering if I'd ever be with Tony Roberts again, wishing he lived in Richmond instead of a hundred miles to the north. His offering to see me home must mean he liked me. Maybe he was as attracted to me as I was to him, I thought, and couldn't stop smiling as I buttoned my coat.

It didn't take long for us to cross the street, not nearly as long as I'd have liked. The night was much cooler than the day had been, and the quarter moon made a bright arc in the sky.

"Do you baby-sit often for Margaret and Richard?" he asked as we reached my yard.

"Some. I'm very fond of Tessa and Timmy, so taking care of them doesn't seem like work. They're well behaved and don't give me problems the way a few other kids have." I sucked my breath in deeply. "How long will you be here, Tony?"

"If tomorrow's weather is good, I'll go back to the dig for a while."

Take me with you to the dig, I begged silently as if I could will him to do it. Please take me with you.

"I really should get home by late tomorrow afternoon in time for some studying," he continued. "It's senior thesis time, and I have a good bit more research to do before I start writing."

"Senior thesis? That's a new one. We don't have those in Richmond."

"Maybe you call them term papers, Beth-Ann."

"Now I know what you're talking about." I laughed, and made a face to indicate that I dreaded the assignment. "Yes, we have term papers. Juniors and seniors have to do them. I think 'senior thesis' sounds a lot more sophisticated. A lot more grim, too."

For a moment neither of us spoke. We were walking more slowly than when we left the Cantrells, and the silence swirled around us. I was dumbfounded to hear myself say, "Tony, I wish you could be in Richmond longer."

"Me, too. But it's impossible this weekend. It was fun meeting you tonight."

We were inches from my front door and the crazy thought hit me that he might kiss me. It was a hope. If he'd attempted it, I wouldn't have objected, despite our having known one another only a few hours.

He didn't. He didn't even give an indication that he'd considered it. I knew my imagination was playing games with my common sense. Besides, our porch light was blazing, blotting out the soft moonlight. As I reached for the doorknob, Tony took a step backwards. He was ready to leave since he had deposited me safely at my house, and there was nothing for me to do but murmur good-night.

My parents were in the living room watching a television movie and before I could ask the question Mom said, "Kenny didn't phone or drop by, Beth-Ann. You really must get in touch with him tomorrow."

Dad, frowning slightly, opened his mouth and closed it without speaking. I had the feeling he'd been about to tell Mom I didn't have to contact Kenny unless I wanted to do it, and then changed his mind about making a comment. Maybe he was tired of discussing what happened between Kenny and me. Sometimes my mother could get wound up on a particular subject and talk about it endlessly.

Both of them glanced at me and I had to reply. "I — uh — I'll think about it," I managed, and faked a yawn. "I'll call it a day now."

They said, "Good-night," in unison and focused their attention on the television screen again. It was a relief not to have to answer further questions.

I suppose I could have told them about meeting Tony, but I didn't. Kenny had slipped to the back of my mind while I was at the Cantrell house, and Tony was the reason. But when I was at home once more, the events of the afternoon came rushing back and a familiar choking sensation made my throat muscles hurt. I bolted away from my parents.

Once in my room, I didn't undress immediately. Without turning on a light, I took a seat on the side of the bed and gazed through the window at the moon that had looked warm and radiant a few minutes earlier when Tony and I were crossing the street.

Dating a boy like Tony Roberts would be heaven, I mused. Not just because he was handsome and charming, but because we shared an interest in history. I liked other things about him, too: the way he showed affection for Tessa, and promised to play with her on Sunday; the genuineness of the big hug he gave his sister; his quiet sense of humor, and his manners.

But Tony lived in northern Virginia, a hundred miles from Richmond, and he hadn't given a single hint that he would like to be with me again. Not one.

Unable to keep still, I got up from the bed and walked over to the desk in the semi-dark room. If Tony had intended to contact me in the future, he would have said something about it. He probably had a girl in Falls Church — maybe many girls. No doubt all of them were beautiful. Smart, too, and loaded with sex appeal. I wouldn't measure up.

Looking at the moon again, I willed myself not to cry from disappointment over Tony and Kenny. Tears wouldn't help; I was very much aware of that. I closed the drapes, turned on the bedside lamp and began to undress, reflecting ruefully that after a grand evening with Tony, I knew exactly how Cinderella felt when she came home from the ball.

Eight

Monday arrived too quickly. I dreaded going to school because it meant facing Kenny, and I didn't know what to expect from him. Would he corner me and resume our quarrel as if no time had passed since Saturday afternoon? Would he be pleasant and act as if nothing had come between us? Would he apologize?

And whatever he did, how should I respond?

I didn't know and was nervous about it. He didn't contact me on Sunday and in spite of my mother's urging, I'd made no effort to get in touch with him.

The sun had been shining when I woke up Sunday morning and I ran to the window, hoping Tony's car would be at the Cantrell's. It wasn't; he must have left for the dig.

I moped around the house, trying to pretend I wasn't staying near the phone, although I was. Tony might call me, I thought, hoping, indulging in wishful thinking. Or, Kenny might. It was easy to fool myself.

Twice during the day I phoned Fran, but the first time no one answered at her house, and later in the afternoon, her mother said she was out with Jack. I should have known. Going to our front windows several more times, I looked across the street and wished Mrs. Cantrell would ask me to baby-sit that evening. It would give me a chance to see Tony — if he was still in the Richmond area. But she didn't, and Tony's car never reappeared. The afternoon dragged on.

While Dad, Mom, and I were having dinner, Mom said, "Don't you plan to apologize to Kenny, Beth-Ann?"

Dad gave her a hard look before I could reply. "I thought we agreed that subject is closed, Lois," he snapped. "If Beth-Ann is old enough to go out with a boy, she's old enough to deal with the situation."

Mom pouted a little, but she hushed. Kenny wasn't mentioned again Sunday night.

Fran and I walked to school together Monday morning, and she was full of chatter. "I didn't see you all weekend," she said. "Where did you and Kenny go? Jack and I ate spaghetti at La Pasta Saturday night, and went to his brother's apartment yesterday to watch TV. That apartment is so romantic. Cozy and dim. . . ." She rolled her eyes. "What about you and Kenny?"

I drew a long breath, feeling the air go all the way to my lungs, and told her what happened. "I don't know what our current set-up is," I added. "I guess I'll find out as soon as we get to school."

"What did you say to turn him off so completely?" she asked. "There must be more than you've told me."

"The Williamsburg bit started it, but I guess my comments about going to a shopping center again got to him."

"Sugar catches more flies than vinegar, Beth-Ann. You were asking for trouble."

Bristling, I almost said she sounded just like my mother, automatically blaming me. But school was in sight and I kept quiet. Her attitude was upsetting, but I wanted to keep my cool. Students were milling about and I didn't want to make a spectacle of myself.

As Fran and I entered the building I saw Kenny in the distance, coming toward us from the far end of the corridor. I felt as if ice cubes were lodged in my chest. Suddenly it hurt to breathe.

Fran saw him, too. "I'll get lost," she whispered and dashed off. I knew she wanted Kenny and me to be by ourselves. Students were everywhere, but that wasn't the same as having a close friend listening to what he and I said to each other.

It wouldn't have made a bit of difference

if she had lingered. Kenny walked past me and muttered hello and kept going. His eyes were focused straight ahead and he didn't glance at me any more than if I'd been a lamppost or a garbage can.

I was shocked. Somehow I hadn't anticipated that, and for a few seconds I couldn't move. I stood in the hall, my coat still buttoned to my chin, my books in the curve of my left arm, my feet welded to the floor.

"Are you okay, Beth-Ann?" a boy's voice asked. The sound of my name brought me out of my daze to recognize Curtis Donovan, a tall, lanky guy, who was taking books from his locker, which was located only three or four feet to the right of where I was standing. I didn't know Curtis well. He'd flunked math back in the ninth grade and when he repeated the course, we were in the same math class since I was a year behind him. He was now a senior, so we hadn't had a class together since then. I don't think we'd ever had much of a conversation.

There was a curious expression on his face as he stared in my direction. If he'd heard Kenny's remark, I didn't see how he could read anything into it, but maybe my face showed consternation.

I made myself speak. "Hello, Curtis," I said in a voice that had a hollow, far-off sound. Without waiting to say more, I started to my homeroom, hurrying so fast I was practically running.

My relationship with Kenny had been

made clear; I now knew where I stood with him. Kenny was the first boy I'd ever dated, the first and only boy I'd ever kissed, and for a short time he had meant everything in my life. All of that was over. Apparently we wouldn't even be friends, if his icy greeting was an indication.

I was numb. The odd aspect is that it didn't hurt as much as I had expected. When I thought about everything later I had some regrets for not acting differently, although I wasn't sure what "differently" implied. At that moment, as I hurried down the school hall, I was more angry than distressed. Kenny could have been polite enough to meet my eyes, I thought bitterly, and a new thought began to nag at me. Had he been ready for us to break up, and was looking for an excuse? I didn't know.

Fran called me late Monday afternoon to ask about my status with Kenny. "I'd have cornered you at school after you saw him this morning, but I was afraid we'd be overheard," she said. "Did you two make up?"

I looked at my hand holding the telephone so hard the skin stretched tightly over my muscles. "Definitely not," I sighed.

"Beth-Ann, I'm sorry."

"I am, too, in a way. But in another way . . . well, I don't know. After all the mean things he and I said Saturday, I guess a clean break is best."

"Did he apologize?"

"No."

"Did you?"

"I didn't say anything. He didn't give me a chance, but it doesn't matter. I doubt if I'd have apologized."

She waited a moment and offered advice. "Get another guy on the double, Beth-Ann. That's the standard cure for a broken heart."

"My heart isn't broken. Cracked a little, but not broken." I gave a choppy, mirthless laugh. "As far as getting another guy is concerned, you know how long it took me to get involved with Kenny. I probably won't have another date until I'm twenty-five years old — if then. I — "

I stopped talking as the door of Mom's car slammed outside. "Fran, I'd better hang up," I said quickly. "My mother is coming in, and I'm not anxious for her to hear me discussing this, because she thinks I ought to call Kenny and beg him to forgive me. I didn't do anything to him but disagree, and make a suggestion — those aren't crimes in my book."

We said hasty good-byes, but I was stupid to think my mother would avoid questions. Maybe she'd have kept silent about Kenny if Dad had been at home, but he hadn't arrived from work. Before she was all the way in the living room, she wanted to know if Kenny and I were on good terms.

"If you mean, will we still date?" I measured each word carefully. "It's doubtful. In fact, the answer is a big, fat no."

She tossed her coat and purse on a chair,

and jerked her head in annoyance. "Beth-Ann Hughes, I'd like to turn you over my knees and spank you as if you were about five years old!" she stormed. "Don't you care about dating? Weren't you happier going with Kenny than when you used to be by yourself, sitting home all the time? Honestly, I don't know what you're thinking about to — "

"Mom, please," I interrupted her. "Can't we drop it? Kenny and I are finished. F-i-n-i-s-h-e-d." I spelled the word. "Haven't you ever broken up with a boy? Don't you know that when it's over, it's over?"

She didn't answer instantly and to my amazement, a few of the tight lines around her mouth softened. "Yes, I suppose I do," she said slowly, her tone almost natural again. "I won't say any more about it. Your father told me I shouldn't get involved, but I want so much for you to be happy and for your teen years to be good ones."

"I know you do," I murmured, and hoped that was the permanent end of our discussion of Kenny Chapman. A car braked in front of our house and Dad's footsteps sounded on the sidewalk. I was eternally thankful he'd come home at that moment.

Nine

It didn't take long for people at school to become aware that Kenny and I were no longer dating, since we didn't sit together in the cafeteria or walk down the hall holding hands. We didn't speak to each other, except to utter terse hellos when it was absolutely necessary. I suppose he was avoiding me as much as I tried to keep away from him.

Fran may have passed the word that the big Chapman-Hughes romance was definitely over because by the middle of the week following the breakup she told me a few questions had been asked. She and I were in the kitchen at my house sitting at the counter drinking Cokes after school. Jack had gone downtown with a group of boys to put in applications for summer jobs.

"Who asked what?" I demanded after her revelation about questions. "Why did they ask you and not me?"

"Get with it, Beth-Ann! You know how it is. Everybody gossips a little, but most people shy away from direct questions." She named two girls I knew casually, Monica Hodges and Katie Wells, and said they wanted to find out every detail of what happened between Kenny and me.

"What did you tell them?" I asked in a thick voice.

"Nothing. I fibbed that I didn't know."

"Thanks." I must have looked relieved. I certainly felt like that.

Laughing, she said, "I think Monica has her eyes on Kenny. She probably was thrilled to hear you'd bowed out of his life."

"I wish her luck," I mumbled sarcastically. "She'll need it."

"Hasn't anybody said anything about it to you, Beth-Ann?"

"Just one person and she didn't ask questions. Vicki Burt told me when we were dressing after gym that she'd been thinking about me 'after what happened.' I thanked her and the bell rang so that was that. But knowing Vicki, she wasn't trying to get a blow-by-blow of Kenny's and my fight; she was just being nice." I took another swallow of Coke and set the red and white can on the counter. "I'm trying to forget about it, Fran, and I hope you'll do the same."

"I'll try. That's a promise. Do you have plans for this weekend?"

"Not at the moment. Maybe something exciting will turn up." My voice was filled with hope. Maybe Tony Roberts will come back to Richmond, I was thinking, but I didn't say it aloud. I hadn't mentioned Tony to anyone.

"Something exciting like a movie star phoning you from Hollywood, or a long lost relative you've never heard of dying and leaving you a few million dollars?" she asked.

She giggled and I joined in. "Why not?" I came back. "If I'm going to dream, I may as well dream big."

Both of us knew that sort of stuff wouldn't happen, but it kept us from dwelling on more serious topics.

The weekend was a dud. There weren't any fun activities for me, but maybe some good came from it because I had the chance for a little serious thinking about myself before Monday morning.

Richmond's taste of spring vanished that weekend, and winter returned. A cold, drizzling rain began Friday and continued through Sunday. It wasn't surprising not to find Tony's car parked across the street. His dig would be impossible in the wet weather. I wondered why I'd assumed that if he returned to Williamsburg, he would automatically stop in Richmond, deciding somewhat wryly that I was getting to be a master at wishful thinking.

After a Sunday afternoon as uninteresting as Saturday had been, I agreed to baby-sit for seven-year-old Roger Baylor that evening. It would give me a chance to get out of the house, away from Mom's I-told-you-what-would-happen-if-you-didn't-make-up-with-Kenny sideways glances in my direction. She didn't mention Kenny by name, but I was sure she was thinking about him.

All weekend I hoped for a call from Mrs. Cantrell since that might give me an opportunity to learn a little more about Tony, but the Cantrells were apparently staying in. Baby-sitting for Roger was a mistake. I suspected in advance it would be, as he was undisciplined. He threw toys from one room to another, sometimes striking the walls or scarring the furniture. Once he even hit my leg with a plastic truck. When I stopped him, and later when I told him not to walk on the back of the sofa, he snarled, "You can't make me! You're not my ma!"

"I'll tell your parents you didn't obey," I said, trying to frighten him into being more cooperative since coaxing and ordering had failed.

"They don't care what I do," he replied smugly.

That had to be the truth. During the Christmas holidays I'd vowed to myself never to sit for him again, and after that Sunday I was positive I'd never return to the Baylor house no matter how much his parents begged or offered to pay.

* * *

Trying to cope with Roger was exhausting, but once I was at home Sunday night I was too keyed up to sleep even though it was nearly midnight. Rain drummed steadily against the roof and outside my bedroom window the sky was completely black. As I got into bed, I went over the events of the last couple of months in my mind. Mom had been correct about one thing: Dating was better than staying by myself. But if I wanted to date again — and I did — I knew I was going to have to change some of my ways.

Rolling over, I plumped the pillow and closed my eyes, my mind racing. I needed to be friendlier, I decided. I thought about Vicki, who was everybody's friend, and planned to be more like her. I would make a point of talking with any boy, or girl, who gave me the slightest opportunity. It could be awkward at first, until I was more accustomed to chatting with boys, but it was worth a try. Holding back and being withdrawn might be my nature, but those traits hadn't brought me any pleasure. After all, I mused, I hadn't been withdrawn with Tony. He and I had hit it off beautifully.

Tony — just thinking his name sent a lovely little shiver up my spine. I refused to permit myself to dwell on him, and continued the frank look at myself.

Was I so eager to date, so eager to feel loved, that I'd given Kenny the idea I was his slave? Because I hadn't questioned our activities until the final Saturday, did he feel I'd never object?

If that was true, I had been too immature to know it. Small wonder he was totally surprised when I made the Williamsburg suggestion, especially when I added that I didn't want to spend any more time in a shopping mall. Before then, I'd always gone along with whatever Kenny wanted.

My bedroom was cool, but my forehead felt feverishly warm as I went over all of it in my mind. In the future when I date I'll be smarter, I told myself. I promptly wondered whether I should use *if* rather than *when*. Maybe I wouldn't have any more dates, maybe boys wouldn't want to waste time with me.

Staring at the dark ceiling, I realized every muscle in my body was tense. The rain had slowed, although it was still falling, and from off in the distance a siren sounded faintly. Sleep was a long time coming.

Ten

My friendliness campaign, if it could be called a "campaign," began the next morning. Fran was at home with a virus that Monday and I walked to school alone. I discovered Curtis Donovan at his locker as soon as I entered the building and it was necessary for me to pass him. I refused to let myself think about the fact that he and I were standing exactly where we'd been the previous Monday, a week earlier, when Kenny ignored me.

Pausing near Curtis, I gave a self-conscious smile and said, "Hi," aware that in the past I'd merely nodded to him without stopping or speaking.

"Hi, yourself." He had a surprised expression. He continued to shuffle through books and papers on the shelf of his locker, although he kept his eyes on me. The silence was painful. I didn't move, even though my mind was blank, and I couldn't think of anything to say.

He grinned and commented, "You seem darn chipper for a Monday, Beth-Ann."

"Isn't everybody?" I came back airily, amazed that I could give a flip reply.

Fran would have been at ease with chatter like that, but I wasn't. I longed to run away from Curtis, to find a dark corner, to do anything except try to force a conversation. But I refused to let myself leave; I'd mapped the campaign and intended to carry it out.

The only way I could have any kind of conversation with him was to ask a question, and I inquired if he had plans for after his graduation in June.

"Nothing definite," he said. "Maybe I'll join the Navy. One thing is for certain — " he shut the locker door and turned toward me " — I don't want to go to college. Not at the present. I've had my fill of school for the time being."

He fell into step with me and we went down the hall together, not touching, just moving in unison. I almost asked if he was aware that he'd have plenty of classes if he enlisted in the Navy — that it would be school under another name — then changed my mind about it. With so much noise around us while the corridor filled up with students, my silence wasn't apparent — at least I hoped it wasn't.

When we reached the door of my homeroom, he said, "See you, Beth-Ann." He probably didn't hear my okay as he spotted two boys, seniors, and yelled to them. I drew a long breath, proud of myself for following through with the campaign. It would have been easier to nod to Curtis and move past him without stopping. I hadn't set out to make a play for Curtis Donovan; he simply was the first boy I saw.

During that Monday I had several other conversations, some with boys, others with girls. I forced myself to make an effort to be outgoing, smiling endlessly. By the final bell I didn't know whether to feel good or bad about the campaign. I was trying, I reminded myself, that was the important part.

Chatting briefly with Curtis before the start of classes grew into a daily routine, and by Thursday it dawned on me he was deliberately hanging around his locker until I reached school. Fran, who was over her virus and back in class on Tuesday, made a crack about it Thursday morning when she and I saw Curtis waiting. She asked slyly if I'd set my sights on him as a replacement for Kenny.

I gave a snort, my face burning. "No. Of course not," I said. I hadn't told anyone about my campaign, not even Fran.

"Don't kid me." She lowered her voice to a whisper as we neared Curtis. "I've seen the way he looks at you lately. I'll bet he asks you for a date before this time next week."

Without letting me answer, she dashed away, and I stopped at Curtis's locker. I no longer had to make myself do it. He seemed glad to see me and that gave me a pleasant sensation.

Friday was when everything changed. At noon Vicki drew me aside when we were leaving the cafeteria, and invited me to a chili supper at her house Saturday night.

"It's not a formal party, so wear jeans or whatever," she said. "I just thought it would be fun to have four or five couples over, and my mother makes fabulous chili."

Going to a party, especially at Vicki's, sounded wonderful; but I hesitated, embarrassed. Her mention of couples made me acutely aware of not having a date for Saturday. Besides, what if Tony Roberts came to Williamsburg Saturday, and stopped in Richmond Saturday night? I'd miss seeing him if I wasn't at home.

That was such a big *if* I shoved it out of my mind. Almost two weeks had gone by since the night Tony was at his sister's, and I'd heard nothing from him. It was silly to think he'd want to be with me even if he visited Mr. and Mrs. Cantrell.

The idea of the chili supper was appealing. Still, there was my dateless condition. Vicki was looking at me so curiously, I realized she was waiting to find out whether or not I'd be at her house.

"I'd love to come," I said, "but maybe I'd better ask for a raincheck. I don't have a date for tomorrow night."

"No matter, Beth-Ann. I'll ask Whit to pick you up."

Whit Markham was a good friend of Kenny's. A lump as big as a walnut rose in my throat.

"I — I — . . Aren't you and W — Whit d — dating?" I inquired shakily.

"We're just good friends. I see a lot of him, but you know I don't go steady. I don't plan to do it until after I graduate. My older sister, who's in college now, had a bad experience going steady when she was in high school — I don't want the misery she had. Tomorrow night I'll be with Chris Abernathy. You'll come, won't you?"

I nodded, wondering what her sister's experience had been. I didn't ask and she didn't explain. Before I could speak, she said, "Oh, by the way, Beth-Ann, don't worry about seeing Kenny tomorrow night. According to Whit, Kenny is leaving after school today to spend the weekend in Raleigh with his grandfather."

"That's okay — I mean, it doesn't matter." It was a lie. Until that instant I hadn't thought about being in the same room with Kenny for hours, but the prospect horrified me. "I — I guess Kenny and I will bump into each other eventually," I said. "It's no big deal."

"You have the right attitude, Beth-Ann. See you tomorrow night at seven."

If Vicki knew I wasn't telling the truth, she'd never have thought I had a good attitude. I hoped I could live up to her opinion. We separated at the cafeteria door, and I realized the tempo of my breathing had increased. It was a relief to know I wouldn't be sitting home alone on Saturday night.

Vicki's invitation wasn't the only unexpected incident that Friday. At the end of school Fran left with Jack as usual, and I was walking home by myself, when a sleek yellow sports car pulled up beside me and Curtis Donovan leaned out of the window.

"Hey," he called and grinned. "Want a ride?"

My eyes widened in astonishment. I had no idea where Curtis lived, but I'd never seen him in my neighborhood so his home had to be in a different part of Richmond. I wondered if he just happened to ride down my street, or if he'd planned it in advance to be with me — the possibility was enchanting.

"My house is only three blocks from here, but I'd love a ride," I told him, finding it easy to return his smile as I took a seat beside him. "Beautiful car, Curtis."

"You like my wheels, huh?"

"How could anyone not like this car?"

"I like it, too." He grinned once more. "I'll reward you for your good judgment by buying you a burger. How about it?"

I said yes and he headed for a fast food place that's popular with kids from our school. The restaurant had a drive-in window. When he suggested we get food there and eat in the car, I murmured, "Fine." Anything would have been all right with me. I was too excited just being near him to be hungry, but I sipped a Coke while he ate a double hamburger with French fries.

Curtis was in a critical frame of mind. His burger was overcooked, he said, and the potatoes were greasy. Cold, too. He griped about weekend homework assignments. He even complained about the arrival of April, saying he hated days when you didn't know whether or not to carry a raincoat.

"Think positively," I came back and laughed. "Maybe this wasn't your best day, but it's Friday. No school tomorrow."

"You have a point, Beth-Ann. You — "

Before he finished whatever he was about to say, Chip Alderson and Barry Smith, seniors at our school, got out of a car parked several spaces away and sauntered over to us. They stopped at Curtis's open window. I knew them casually and all of us said hello. The boys sent dumb jokes back and forth until Barry said, "Want to hear a good joke?"

"Sure," Curtis answered. "Hey, Barry, hold it! I know your kind of jokes and Beth-Ann might not go for them. Save it for later."

"Aw, come on," Barry said. "This one is great."

I didn't know whether I was supposed to

object or urge him to tell the joke. I did nothing, hoping I wasn't blushing, although I must have looked embarrassed since Chip piped up with, "Save it for later, Barry."

"No way. I might forget the punch line." Barry walked a short distance from the car, motioning for Curtis and Chip to join him. To my dismay, they did.

I sat very still by myself in the yellow car, staring at the ice in the bottom of my paper cup. In a moment all three boys guffawed loudly before leaning forward, their heads close together. Chip was talking that time. I heard the mumble of voices without understanding the words. It was obvious they were deep into another joke.

I jiggled the few drops of melted ice around in my cup, thinking how ugly the watery brown liquid, part Coke and part water, appeared. Ten minutes went by, then another five minutes. A feeling of annoyance was growing in me. The boys continued to stand some twenty feet away from the car, chuckling among themselves.

"Curtis, it's after five o'clock and I have to go home," I called.

He looked at his watch, glanced in my direction and saluted, then ambled back to the car. Chip and Barry crossed the parking lot to their car.

"Want to scare up some action tomorrow night, Beth-Ann?" Curtis said as he started the engine.

He was asking for a date! My annoyance

vanished. Two date opportunities for one evening — that had never happened to me before and I could only accept one.

"Thanks, Curtis, but I already have plans for tomorrow night," I replied, and hoped my voice didn't sound as exhilarated as I felt. I didn't want him to know how inexperienced I was.

He muttered, "Hell," under his breath before saying, "Okay, what about tonight? We can see a movie or something?"

"Love it." I laughed out loud from sheer happiness.

Dinner was on the table when I reached home and I deliberately waited until we finished eating to mention going out so Mom wouldn't have the chance to ask a lot of questions. She gave Curtis the once-over when he came for me, smiling because there was a new guy in my life. Dad was frankly critical in the way he stared at Curtis when the two of them shook hands. I broke that up by saying we were going to the early movie and got Curtis out of the house in a hurry.

I was a little embarrassed by Curtis's appearance. I'd taken a shower and put on a fresh blouse with my best skirt, a green and bronze plaid that I seldom wore to school, and taken pains with my makeup. Curtis hadn't even bothered to wash his face since a mark from a ballpoint pen that I'd noticed on his cheek earlier was still there. He wore the same, rather dilapidated red sweat shirt he'd had on all day. I hadn't expected him to wear a coat and tie, but I thought he'd clean up a bit.

The movie wasn't as good as its advance notices and when we left the theater, Curtis began to gripe the way he'd done in the afternoon. The acting was lousy and the plot was dull, he maintained. I didn't feel it was all that bad, though it would never win any awards. But Curtis's gripes didn't stop there — he thought the popcorn was too salty, despite eating an entire box. And he said so much about how expensive movie tickets were, that I was embarrassed at what he'd spent.

Since we'd gone to the early show, it was only half past nine when we returned to the yellow car. He made no attempt to turn on the ignition immediately.

"What do you want to do now?" he asked. "Is the coast clear at your house?"

I was about to say I'd pay for a snack since he'd bought food in the afternoon and taken care of the tickets, but his question didn't sound as if he was hungry. If our house only had a den, I thought just as I used to do when Kenny and I had dated.

"If you mean are my parents at home, I'm afraid they will be," I said. "But you and I won't have to stay in the living room with them. We can go in the kitch — "

"What about your room?" he cut in. "You

don't have a roommate, do you? If you bunk with a kid sister, maybe I can bribe her not to hang around."

"No roommate." I attempted a laugh and it came out as a raspy noise. "But no dating in the bedroom, that's one of my family's rules."

I thought he'd protest, but he only shrugged. "My house isn't exactly available, either," he said, and strummed his fingers on the steering wheel. "Where can we go for a little privacy? Any suggestions?"

We were still sitting in the car in the theater parking lot and the lights from the sign over the box office illuminated the interior of the automobile. I hoped I didn't look as ill at ease as I felt.

"I'm waiting for you to get a brainstorm," he went on. "Where can we go to have some action?"

"S— some action?" I stammered.

"Sure. Why not?" Taking his hands off the wheel, he swiftly reached for me, pulled me close and kissed me painfully hard on the lips. It took me by surprise and I twisted away, conscious of the lights and how conspicious we were in a public place.

"What gives?" he demanded. "Don't you like the way I kiss?"

"I do, but —" I didn't know whether I liked it or not.

"What's wrong with you, Beth-Ann? I spent plenty on you this afternoon and tonight, and I ought to rate some action in return!"

A sour taste came into my mouth. It dawned on me I didn't actually know Curtis Donovan. A few moments of chitchat before the start of classes didn't indicate what sort of person he was, anymore than it told him about me.

"Are you just going to sit there like a zombie?" He was irked and it showed. "Can't you speak?"

"I — I'm n — not sure what you m — mean by 'some action,' Curtis."

The look he gave me would have melted iron. "If you have to ask, you're definitely not my type," he growled, and started the motor.

"Maybe I'm not," I managed, my jaws clenched. "I think I'd better go home now."

He didn't argue about that. Pressing his foot hard on the accelerator, he whirled around corners until we reached my house. He put on brakes but didn't cut off the engine or make any effort to get out of the car.

"Thanks for the movie," I said and stepped to the ground.

"The next time you lead a guy on like you've done to me all week, Beth-Ann, don't build him up to something big and then let him down with a thud. Okay?"

I opened my mouth and no words came. Turning away from him, I ran to the house without replying. Behind me, I heard him speed off.

Had I led him on? The question burned into my brain. In a way, maybe I had with those before-class stops to talk to him. But I didn't believe I'd done anything to make him feel I wanted what he called "some action." Was his idea of "action" a lot of kissing? The one grabbing embrace and kiss he'd given me in the theater parking lot hadn't brought me any pleasure. It was a shock to realize I didn't want him to kiss me again. I'd fancied myself in love with Kenny when he and I shared kisses, but love hadn't entered into my relationship with Curtis. I knew at that moment how little a kiss meant if there was no caring.

If Curtis expected sex when he mentioned "action," he should have known my answer would be *No* with a capital *N*.

The outside light by our front door was burning, as usual. I hurried inside, sending up a silent prayer that my parents would be in their room so I wouldn't have to explain about coming home from a date a few minutes after ten o'clock, but I wasn't that lucky. They were seated side by side on the sofa watching television, and both of them were surprised to see me.

"Something wrong, Beth-Ann?" Dad inquired at once.

"Wrong?" I was stalling, trying to come up with a satisfactory reply, and at the same time reveal nothing. The effort I made to smile must have looked as false as it felt.

"What your father means is, did something happen during your date to make you come home this early?" Mom explained, as if I didn't know what Dad was asking.

"No." I tried to sound natural. "Everything is fine."

"Then why did Curtis bring you home so early?" Mom persisted. "Is he coming in?"

I decided to quiet her once and for all where Curtis Donovan was concerned. If I didn't, I could brace myself for a million questions.

"Curtis and I didn't hit it off," I announced flatly. "I didn't really know him because he's a senior and most of his friends are seniors. Tonight I discovered we don't see eye-to-eye on very many things. After the movie ended, it seemed a whole lot better to say good-night and good-bye than to bore one another, or to argue."

Mom started to speak and coughed instead. She sounded as if she'd strangled and I ran to the kitchen to get her a glass of water. Dad was chuckling to himself when I returned. Maybe he guessed what had happened between Curtis and me. I didn't know and at that moment I didn't care.

My mother got her throat cleared and seemed about to begin the questions, but I didn't give her an opportunity. Saying good-night, I practically tripped over my own feet in my hurry to get to my room.

E^{leven}

Saturday began another bad weather weekend. I gave a frustrated sigh when I woke up to the sight and sound of rain, because it meant Tony Roberts wouldn't come to Williamsburg, and to Richmond.

I turned on the radio, then tried television, but the Saturday morning programs were designed for little kids. I put a slice of bread in the toaster and poured a glass of juice. I was delighted when Fran called.

"If you're not doing anything important, I'll come over," she said. "Mom is heading for the supermarket, and she can drop me off at your house in a few minutes."

"The most important thing I'm doing is getting ready to eat toast with orange marmalade," I replied. "I'll give you some if you want."

"Please don't. I've already had breakfast

and besides, I need to lose five pounds. See you shortly."

Fran didn't even wait to get her raincoat off before asking, "Did you do anything exciting last night? What I want to know is, did Kenny call you by any chance?"

I made a face at her. "Kenny Chapman is definitely past tense in my life. As to last night, it depends on what you describe as 'exciting.' I had a date with Curtis Donovan."

She squealed and wagged her forefinger at me. "Didn't I tell you Curtis was going to ask you for a date? I knew he would. How was everything? What did you and Curtis do? Is this the start of a big romance? Was — "

"Slow down and give me a chance, and I'll tell you," I interrupted.

We went into my room and settled ourselves on the bed. Fran sat with her back resting against a pillow propped on the footboard while I was opposite her, sitting crosslegged so that we faced each other. I began to talk about the events of Friday afternoon and evening, telling her everything; starting with Curtis offering me a ride and our stop at the drive-in and winding up with the acid conversation following the movie. For once she didn't interrupt.

"Now you know," I finished, my mouth uncommonly dry. "Curtis and I definitely aren't made for each other. No big romance." I laughed thinly. "To be truthful, nothing."

"You're getting smarter, Beth-Ann."

"Smarter? How?"

"There was a time you'd have dated anybody just to be having a date. But there's no law making you put up with a guy you don't like. Still," she focused her eyes on me, "I think maybe you're too choosy. You could have laughed off Curtis' comments about 'action' and suggested food, or something. You could have started talking a mile a minute about school or the movie, or the weather, or whatever came to mind rather than have the date end unpleasantly. As it is now, he'll never give you the time of day."

"I don't want him to give me the time of day! I won't take up any time with him, either."

"Boys talk. He could ruin your chances with other guys if he told them you were no fun."

"Maybe I'm not any fun."

"Beth-Ann, you used to feel bad because you didn't date, and now you're irked because you can't program boys like they're computers."

That was too much. "You're wrong!" I came back defensively. "I don't consider them to be dummies for me to boss! But just once I want to be with a boy who likes what I like! Is that so weird?"

"No, it's not weird, but you're asking a lot. While you're waiting for Superman to come whizzing in, don't turn into a snob."

"I am not a snob!" I said hotly, on the defensive again. "I thought you were my friend and you're saying awful stuff to me."

"I *am* your friend. That's why I don't want you to get the reputation at school for being a snob. You might if you keep on breaking up with every guy you date."

The fire went out of me. "I really am not a snob," I sighed. "At least, I don't think I am, and I don't mean to give that impression. I don't expect every boy to be perfect, either. But there are a lot of interesting things to do and see, and the guys I've dated don't want to try any of them. I don't want every date to be sitting in a shopping mall, or riding around until we find a place where a lot of the guy's friends are congregated. My idea of a good time isn't waiting in the car watching guys swap dirty jokes."

"I sure don't blame you for that."

We were silent a few seconds. She traced the woven design in my blue and white bedspread with her finger.

"Sounds to me as if you know the wrong guys," she said finally.

"Maybe I do. Wrong for me, anyway." I thought of Tony who would have been very right for me, but I didn't mention him to Fran. With a twisted smile, I tossed her a question to get the conversation away from my situation. "How did you know Jack was right for you?"

"We just sort of clicked. Instinct, I guess. Do you have plans for tonight?"

When I told her about Vicki's party, she positively purred. "Mmmmmm, Whit Mark-

127

ham." She gave a thumb's up sign. "Give me a report later on how you like him. I've always thought he seemed like a truly nice guy."

"Don't start putting two and two together and making four, Fran. Remember Whit didn't ask me. Vicki said she'd arrange for him to bring me; there's a difference."

"Well, turn on all your charm. Maybe next time he'll arrange his own date with you."

Maybe, I thought, not saying the word aloud. My self-confidence about dating had been damaged and I didn't know whether to believe it actually would happen or not.

It was a relief when Whit phoned late in the afternoon to say he'd pick me up. I'd been nursing a big fear that Vicki might have forgotten to give him the message, or that he'd simply decided not to bother, but I needn't have worried.

The Burts' recreational room was as inviting as it appeared the first time I saw it. The red sofas were lovely and the log fire on the hearth gave off just enough warmth to take the chill out of the damp spring evening. Whit and I arrived to find Vicki's date, Chris Abernathy, already there, and so were Katie Wells and Zach Lacy, students at our school. I was amazed at the wideness of Vicki's circle of friends. Her cousin, a stunning redhead named Theresa from Petersburg, a town twenty-eight miles south of Richmond, came in with a date from the same community.

They attended high school, too, and all of us laughed and chatted as if we were longtime friends.

Mrs. Burt's chili was as fabulous as Vicki said it would be. We had a big green salad with it, followed by caramel cake for dessert. After we ate, we turned the stereo on and danced. When the party broke up, I meant it when I told Vicki I'd had a marvelous time.

"Me, too," Whit chimed in, grinning at her over my shoulder.

Knowing Whit was a special friend of Kenny's, I'd braced myself to feel ill at ease with him. But it didn't happen, not even when just the two of us were alone in his car. He pulled up to my house and said, "I had a nice time, Beth-Ann. I hope we can get together again."

"So do I," I replied.

He walked with me to the house and waited in the circle of light while I searched in the bottom of my purse for the key. I didn't expect a good-night kiss. He didn't attempt to give me one, and I was glad. A kiss, I'd already decided privately, should mean something, and not simply be a routine. Whit and I knew one another too casually for kisses.

After I fitted the key into the lock, I turned to say good-night to him. He was smiling.

"I'll call you," he said softly. "Soon."

Somehow I knew he would, and I wanted him to do it.

Twelve

The rain stopped Sunday afternoon, although the sky remained a dark, murky gray. I was conscious of an inner restlessness that wasn't to be blamed entirely on the weather. The truth was I couldn't get Tony Roberts out of my thoughts.

Standing by the window in my room, I gazed out at the soggy landscape and made a snap decision: I'd go visit the Cantrells. Their car was in front of their house, so I knew they were at home and maybe, just maybe, I'd be able to work Tony's name into the conversation. I felt as if I'd explode any second if I couldn't find out something about him.

Because I didn't want the reason for my visit to be obvious, I looked around for something to take the Cantrell children. Mom had saved the toys I had when I was a child, and in the attic I found an envelope of paper dolls with clothes that would be perfect for Tessa. Timmy was a different matter. I had nothing that would appeal to a boy, but several small cardboard boxes of assorted sizes were in a basket near the toys. Timmy could use them like blocks or fit one box into another, I decided. I put them into a brown paper bag for him.

Dad was asleep on the living room sofa as I got my coat. Mom was puttering around the kitchen trying to decide if she would make a chocolate or an apple pie for dinner. She wasn't really into cooking, and it surprised me to find her studying recipes.

"Your father said the other day we hadn't had a homemade dessert in ages, and he's right," she remarked.

"Make apple and use brown sugar. You did that for Dad's birthday instead of making a cake for him and the pie was yummy," I said, and told her where I was heading.

Carefully avoiding the puddles in the street, I saw the Cantrells' door open before I reached their stoop. Tessa was jumping up and down.

"It's Beth-Ann, Mommy!" she said. "Beth-Ann has come to play with me."

Mrs. Cantrell gave me a big welcome. "You couldn't have chosen a better time," she said and smiled. "My husband is upstairs in bed with the flu, and the children and I are getting on each other's nerves."

Tessa was thrilled with the paper dolls, putting various outfits on each one and bringing them to me for my approval. Timmy stacked the boxes into a column and laughed when they toppled over. After a few minutes the youngsters were so engrossed in their playing that Mrs. Cantrell and I had a chance to talk.

She opened her knitting bag and began to work on a skein of yellow yarn, the shiny steel needles clicking as she added stitches to a small garment.

"What's it going to be?" I inquired. "A sweater?"

"Yes, for Tessa. I've already finished a matching one for Timmy. What have you been doing lately, Beth-Ann?"

"Next week is a biggie for me. I start behind-the-wheel driver education," I said. "I've already finished the classroom part of the course and practiced with the simulator; now I'll actually get to drive. It's Monday to Friday for an hour every afternoon after classes."

"So you'll have your license by the end of the school term in June?"

"I hope." I held up both hands, my fingers crossed. "If I pass the test, of course."

"You will, I don't doubt that. What about your dating? Are you seeing the same boy every weekend? Or are you playing the field?"

The knitting needles clicked softly. I could feel myself blushing, especially when she took her eyes off the half-finished sweater to look at me.

"I don't go steady, if that's what you mean," I murmured.

She had brought up the subject of dating and it was my opportunity to find out if Tony had a steady girl, but I couldn't make myself ask the question. This was what I'd wanted, the chance to talk about him, and I was a lump of ice, terrified with fear that I'd give my feelings away if I said his name aloud.

"My younger brother Tony doesn't go steady, either," Mrs. Cantrell said, and I gave a gasp when she mentioned him. "You recall meeting Tony three or four weeks ago, when you were baby-sitting and he popped in without notice, don't you?"

Did I recall? If she only knew.

Miraculously, I found my voice. "Yes, he seemed very nice." That was the understatement of the year.

"He is. Tony's a love." She smiled as she spoke. "He calls himself 'an afterthought' since he's so much younger than the rest of us. There are five children in our family. My parents say he's a bonus. He keeps them young with his activities and interests."

"Is — is he still involved with the W — Williamsburg dig?" I stammered. Blood was thundering in my ears.

"That's his main thing right now. But between the rain and his having to write some sort of thesis, Mama said he hasn't been able to go to Williamsburg recently, but she told me yesterday Tony handed that thesis in last week." She paused, holding the knitting in both hands, the long, gleaming needles crossed in the air. "Beth-Ann, you made a real impression on Tony that night he was here. At breakfast the next morning he asked me several questions about you."

"About me?" The words rolled around in my mouth and all the time I thought, Tell me, tell me.

"He wanted to know if you were tied up with one special boy," she said. "I told him I didn't know, that you must be popular since now it's not always possible for you to baby-sit on weekends since you began dating."

She stopped the knitting stitches, turned the sweater over, and began to purl. I watched, hypnotized by her flying fingers.

"Tony was impressed by your interest in his dig," she went on. "Some of his school friends apparently think that's a dull hobby."

"I don't think it's dull!" The sentence shot out. I didn't mean to speak with such vehemence, and my face felt hot once more. Drawing a long breath, I managed to ask one of the questions that was all-important to me. "When will Tony be back here, Mrs. Cantrell?"

"I don't know. Not until the weekend weather improves, I suppose. I've told him his bed will be available whenever he wants to come. He may have to hold off on the dig for a while, since he'll have final exams in another month, which means studying, and graduation activities. Mama said he's lined up the same lifeguard job for the summer that he had last year. I don't know if that involves his working weekends at the pool or not."

My hopes had been soaring and they sank with a clunk. I seemed to shrivel inside. It could be months and months before I saw Tony Roberts again. In the fall he'd go to college, and might be too far away to visit Richmond, or Williamsburg.

While I was attempting to get myself together, Tessa ran to me with a paper doll dress she'd torn, her eyes spilling tears. I asked Mrs. Cantrell if she had any Scotch tape, assuring the child the dress could be mended and would be fine.

Mrs. Cantrell and I never got back to discussing Tony. I stayed another fifteen minutes and went home.

"Beth-Ann, you had a phone call while you were out," Mom said as I came through the living room to the kitchen. She was lifting the pie from the oven, and the delicious aroma of apples and spices rose from the brown crust.

"Fran?" I asked. "Did she want me to call her back?"

"No, it was a boy. Whit something-or-other. Isn't he the one you went out with last night?"

"Yes, he is." My head was whirling.

It seemed to take my mother a very long time to set the pie on a trivet on the counter, and she didn't speak while she was doing it.

Finally she said, "I told him you'd probably be home between five-thirty and six."

Whit Markham calling me? I had a hard time believing it. My watch showed the time was eleven minutes to six — and the phone rang.

"Remember me, Beth-Ann?" Whit asked, and I had a mental picture of him smiling at the silly question.

"Let's see. Whit Brown? Whit Smith?" I played along. "Oh, I know now, Whit Markham." Both of us laughed.

"Would you be interested in going to the Science Museum tonight to see a program on comets?" he asked. "I'm sorry to be so late asking you, but I only got the tickets a little while ago. Our next door neighbors had planned to attend the program, but both of them have come down with the flu. They called my house an hour ago to say I could use their tickets if I want. It's supposed to be a good show."

"I certainly would, Whit. I'm glad I've already done my homework for Monday."

"Me, too. It begins at eight. Okay if I come for you at seven-thirty?"

Anything would have been okay. I told him I'd be ready and eased the phone back into its cradle, conscious that I was smiling. My gloom over the thought of not seeing Tony in the immediate future had been pushed aside, and all of a sudden, everything was wonderful.

Thirteen

Monday was the start of a busy week for me. The behind-the-wheel driver's ed classes took care of the afternoons. I didn't anticipate how tense I'd be at first; part of that sensation disappeared after a few days, though. The learners' cars had dual controls, so the instructor sat beside me on the front seat. It was comforting to realize that if I made a drastic error, like hitting the accelerator when I should have put my foot on the brake, the teacher could take over and drive the car. But I was so terribly nervous I couldn't relax.

Fran and I talked about it when we were walking to school Monday morning. She was beginning her behind-the-wheel lessons at the same time.

"I wonder if my parents will ever trust me with one of our cars," she sighed. "Mom is already giving me do's and don'ts, and I haven't had the first class yet. She's so up-tight about the idea of my driving, she probably hopes I'll flunk and can't get a license."

I gave her an understanding look. "My parents are sort of the same," I admitted. "I don't believe Mom could ride with me without going into shock. I have the jitters just thinking about goofing when the instructor is telling me what to do."

"Let's talk about something else, Beth-Ann. Tell me about your weekend. Mine was okay, but not spectacular. Jack and I bummed around Regency Mall shopping center Saturday night, and went to the movies Sunday. We saw the film you saw with Curtis, and I agree with you that it wasn't Oscar material."

The day was dazzling with golden sunshine. The yards Fran and I passed glowed with yellow jonquils and early red tulips, and the grass was lushly green. May would arrive shortly, and I was conscious of a wonderful springtime aroma in the balmy air.

As I described Vicki's party, Fran nodded from time to time. She and I had left home earlier than usual and didn't have to hurry, our strides slowing almost to a stroll.

"Why don't you ask about my Sunday night?" I said when I finished talking about the chili supper.

"Don't keep me guessing, Beth-Ann. What happened Sunday night?"

"Whit took me to the Science Musuem."

"Whit Markham asked you for a date after

being with you Saturday! Wow and double wow! That's the most! But — " she caught her breath " — the Science Musuem? Couldn't he find something more exciting than that?"

"It was a fascinating program on comets. We loved it, and I learned a lot."

She gave me a glance that said plainly she thought I was lying. "But wasn't it just like sitting in class at school?" she asked.

"I wish all my classes were that interesting. It only lasted an hour. Both of us could have listened another hour or longer."

"To each his own, as they say." She shifted her books from one arm to the other. "What did you do after the program ended?"

"Came back to my house. Mom had made an apple pie for dessert, and there was plenty left, so Whit and I finished it off. And we talked, of course."

"Were your parents underfoot?"

"They were in the living room, and we were in the kitchen. Whit didn't seem to mind being there. I told him that I wished we had a den, and he said his family only had a living room, too."

"Did he ask for another date?"

"Not a specific one. But he said he'd 'see me,' and we decided to keep an eye on the Science Museum programs; and go to another one. The programs change from time to time."

We were at school. Students were pouring out of the yellow buses parked at the curb, and I was ready to stop talking about Whit's and my date. "Did you have trouble with the math homework?" I asked, changing the subject.

"Wait a sec, Beth-Ann! I haven't found out all I want to know about you and Whit. Did he kiss you good-night?"

"No, and I didn't think he would. He and I are just friends. After all, Mom and Dad were still in the living room when he left."

"'Nuff said." She rolled her eyes and laughed. "About the math, yes, I had trouble with it. Jack did, too. Neither of us could complete the assignment."

There was one part of Whit's and my Sunday night conversation I didn't repeat to Fran, because it seemed too private to discuss with anybody, even my best friend. It happened as he and I finished our pie. I put the empty plates and milk glasses in the sink.

"Want me to wash them?" he asked.

I shook my head. "They'll keep until tomorrow." I was determined not to make him do kitchen work on our first date. I didn't count Saturday night as a real date, since our being together was arranged by Vicki.

"Beth-Ann, there's something I'd like to ask you," Whit said, his voice low. "If it's none of my business, I hope you'll tell me to shut up, but — well, it's something I've been thinking about."

Opening my mouth, I closed it without speaking, unable to come up with a suitable reply. I couldn't imagine what he had on his mind.

He glanced at me and looked down at his square hands with long, blunt fingers. "How serious were you and Kenny before you called it quits?" he blurted out.

I wanted to tell him he was right, that it wasn't his business. But I couldn't do it. I couldn't lie to him, either.

"I — I guess we were serious at first," I managed. "I was, anyway. I don't actually know how he felt. But — but everything ended suddenly. Since then . . . I've tried to analyze my feelings — maybe infatuation would be the best way to describe what we had. It's definitely over."

"That's a relief." He waited a moment and said, "Kenny and I are longtime friends. You know that, don't you?"

I nodded.

"We've been pals as far back as I can remember. That doesn't mean we agree all the time, or think alike. Especially now that we're older, but — " He flung his hands out, palms up. "What I'm leading up to is that I told him Friday morning I planned to ask you for a date. I didn't want any misunderstanding between him and me, in case he intended to date you again."

"What did he say?" My throat was so dry, my tongue seemed stuck to the roof of my mouth.

"Do you want a literal reply?" He grinned

slightly. " 'Feel free.' Those were his very words." Whit's smile deepened. "And I did. I saw Vicki on the way to school Friday, and when she invited me to the chili supper, she said for me to bring any date I wanted. I said I'd like to ask you, and she said she'd already decided to invite you, but she didn't want it to be a bad scene if Kenny was at her house at the same time. The chili party was planned so quickly she hadn't had a chance to contact people, and she was going to do that at school since she was only having a few couples, not a big crowd. I told her I'd talked to Kenny Thursday night, and he and his family were heading for Raleigh to spend the weekend."

"When she invited me, I told her I'd love to come but didn't have a date," I confessed. "I thought the only reason I was with you was because she asked you to bring me."

"Did that make a difference, Beth-Ann?"

"It's nicer to know it was your idea."

Our eyes met. There was a moment of silence that I broke by saying, "I used to think you and Vicki were seriously involved, Whit." I was unable to say "were in love."

"We're longtime friends, just the way Kenny and I are. The three of us used to live on the same block when we were kids. Kenny's folks moved first, then the Burts built their house, and my family stayed put. But Kenny, Vicki and I went to the same grammar school and junior high, now we're in the same high school. Sure, Vicki and I date, but we've never been in love or anything."

"She told me she didn't go steady."

"I don't, either, Beth-Ann. Maybe I'll eat those words as soon as I meet *the girl*. But right now, it's more fun not to be tied down to any one person. I hope you understand."

I said I did, and we were silent once more, until I asked Whit about Vicki's sister. "Vicki told me her sister endured something tragic that was the result of going steady, and I've wondered about it," I said.

He seemed surprised by the question. "Do you know Claudia, Beth-Ann? She's four years older than Vicki."

I shook my head.

"She looks a lot like Vicki. Both of them are super-great. What happened isn't a secret, it was general knowledge, so I'm not betraying a confidence to tell you. Claudia began dating this guy when she was in junior high, and they were inseparable. A real matched pair — you never saw one without the other. By the time they were seniors in high school, everybody thought they might get married immediately after they graduated, and then go to college together. I don't believe their parents would have objected at that point, since both families were friends."

He sucked his breath in. "Would you believe that joker stood Claudia up for a big party about a month before graduation when they were seniors? She was dressed and waiting at her house, and he'd even sent her a corsage. He simply didn't show. Never even called or wrote her to say good-bye."

"Why? Where was he?" I asked.

"That's the unbelievable part, Beth-Ann. After waiting a couple of hours, Claudia phoned his house. His father tried to locate him and couldn't. His parents finally notified the police that he was missing, and it seems he'd joined the army the previous day. He had passed his physical, then went to school that morning as usual. He cut his last class of the day to go back downtown to the recruiting office and left that afternoon on a bus for Fort Bragg with a bunch of other recruits. He was eighteen and could do it without his folks' permission, although he did leave his mother a note. It was hidden under the pillow on his bed, and they didn't find it until several days later when she was changing the sheets. It almost killed Claudia, especially his not telling her — his mother, too. I don't think they'd have objected to his enlisting if he'd waited to graduate, or told them his plans. But the way he did it hurt a lot of people."

"I can imagine." I shuddered at the thought. "Did they ever find out why?"

"I haven't heard an explanation. It was really hard on Vicki, too. It was a year before Claudia was interested in dating again. That's the reason Vicki decided not to go steady, or get seriously involved with any boy until she's older, and I respect her for it.

So does Kenny. He and I are sort of like brothers to her."

"I never saw that side of Kenny," I murmured, wondering if I had misjudged him. Still, Kenny Chapman and I didn't talk seriously. I didn't know much about him except that he was handsome and his kisses made me quiver.

"Kenny is okay, Beth-Ann," Whit said. "He's hotheaded at times, but that's just his personality and I've learned to overlook it." His mouth twisted into a half-grin. "When you and I started on this subject, I told you I didn't mean to pry into your business, but I'm glad we've talked about it. Now I won't feel I'm sticking my neck out and alienating Kenny, or you, if I ask you for a date."

He wanted to see me again! I gave him a radiant smile. "I'm glad we talked about it, too," I said.

Looking at his watch, Whit got to his feet. It was time for him to go, but I hated to see him leave.

"I wish the evening was just beginning," I said. "It's been that much fun."

"I think so, too." He rubbed his fingertips gently against my cheek. For a second I thought he was about to kiss me as we stood in the kitchen, but he didn't. His touch was so light I'd probably have thought I imagined it, if I hadn't seen him drop his hand. It was obvious he liked me, and I hoped he realized I liked him.

That was another matter I didn't intend to discuss with Fran, or anyone else.

Vicki and I ate lunch at the same table at noon that Monday, and I mentioned how much I'd enjoyed the chili supper. After my next class, I was walking down the corridor when Whit fell into step with me.

"Are you all set to master the art of driving a car in one easy lesson this afternoon?" he asked.

"Don't tease me about it," I said tensely. "I'm scared to pieces."

"Scared of what, Beth-Ann?" The mocking note left his voice, and he was serious. "Think about it like learning to swim, or ride a bike, or roller-skate. The first time you try will be rough, just as learning those things was. But eventually you'll get the hang of it, and life will be great. You won't ever forget how to do it, either. People might become a little rusty, but nobody forgets how to skate or swim, or ride a bike — or drive a car."

We reached the stairs. He started up, while my next class was straight ahead.

"Thanks for the encouragement," I told him. "Thanks for taking me to the Science Museum, too."

"I'll call you tonight to find out how you did in driver's ed." He winked in my direction then took the steps two at a time.

Fourteen

When I came home Thursday afternoon I was tired, but wildly excited at the same moment — the two feelings mixed up together. Whit had said I'd get the hang of driving eventually. Privately, I had begun to doubt it during my first three lessons. Fran was assigned to another group. She, as well as the rest of my section, appeared completely at ease behind the steering wheel, but I wasn't.

Until Thursday.

At the start of the first behind-the-wheel class Monday afternoon, the instructor told me what I needed was a teaspoonful of self-confidence. Three or four times during each lesson, he urged me to relax. I tried and couldn't. I was stiff and tense until the miracle happened Thursday. I don't know what caused the change; I just knew everything was different.

On Thursday when I touched the starter button, the engine purred, and the car moved forward without jumping. I managed to maneuver around a corner without slamming on the brakes so hard the motor cut off, and I accelerated smoothly. In a short time I realized I was leaning my back comfortably against the seat, instead of sitting rigidly, as if an iron bar had been forced into my spine. My hands held the wheel in a light way, rather than clawing it in a death grip.

When the lesson ended, I don't think I walked home — I floated, my feet barely touching the sidewalk. For the first time I hadn't wanted to stop driving. I wished the lesson would last for hours.

When I reached home after driver's ed, fatigue hit me and suddenly I was drained.

In my room I stretched out on the bed, and lay there fifteen or twenty minutes, my eyes half closed. At first I wasn't consciously thinking about anything. Gradually as the tension went out of my body, I was aware of how much my life had changed in recent months. I had changed, too. I was more assured, better adjusted. Dating was partly responsible, I felt sure. Now that I could number several boys among my friends and knew more girls, I didn't feel as insecure and unattractive as I had before. I was more willing to be myself, instead of withdrawing into a shell. Fran was still my good friend, but no longer my only friend.

I thought about Whit. He appeared to be

truly interested in my progress, or lack of it, with driver's ed. Maybe I should call him and tell him what had just happened, I mused. Not being in the habit of calling boys, I hesitated. Then I made the decision to do it and looked up his number in the directory.

When he answered, his Hi, Beth-Ann, sounded as if he was surprised to hear from me. I was a little surprised at myself for calling him.

"I wanted to tell you my good news," the words tumbled out. "Today I did what you said I'd do. I finally drove the car like a normal person without driving off the road."

"Great! I knew you'd make it. How do you feel?"

"Triumphant." I gave a low laugh. "Sort of tired, too. But I loved doing it and can't wait for tomorrow's lesson. I think my instructor is secretly relieved. He probably figured he had a hopeless nerd on his hands."

"You'll be ready to race in the Indianapolis 500 before you know it, Beth-Ann. All you needed was time. This calls for a celebration. Want to do something tomorrow night to mark the big event?"

"Love to." I smiled into the phone. My fatigue had gone.

"What about going to Monty's for pizza? Vicki and Chris are dating tomorrow night and if you like, we can make it a foursome."

"I like, Whit. Very much."

"Incidentally, I have a bit of good news of my own. I've got a job, and start work

Saturday." He named a hardware store in a shopping center not far from my neighborhood. "I'll just work Saturdays until school is out in June, but during the summer, I'll put in a five-day week."

"That's wonderful," I told him. "What sort of work will you do?"

"Mostly bring stock from the warehouse and carry heavy merchandise to cars for customers. Maybe I'll have the chance to sell a little, too. I hope so. I worked there during the Christmas holidays, but the business changed hands in January, and I wasn't sure if the new owners would take on students. They will — I was notified this afternoon." He cleared his throat. "There's just one catch."

"Everything has at least one catch," I said, and laughed. "What's yours?"

"For the present, my Saturdays will be long, long work days. I'll be on the job from eight in the mornings until the store closes at ten p.m., which will take care of Saturday night dates. But I'm glad for the extra hours, since I'll only work one day a week until after exams. I can make up for the lack of Saturday night fun with big plans for Fridays and Sundays."

He and I chatted a few more minutes and as we rang off, I heard Mom coming in. She wasn't as impressed with my news about driving as I wanted her to be. She looked tired, and said her day was so rushed she'd worked through the lunch hour, drinking a cup of coffee at her desk instead of eating. She'd feel better after some food, I felt, and that turned out to be correct. We went to a Chinese restaurant, and she perked up after a bowl of egg drop soup and a chicken dish with toasted almonds on top, with an unpronounceable name.

It wasn't until later that evening, after Dad came in and my homework was finished, that I picked up the afternoon newspaper I'd carried into the house earlier. The pictures and news story on the front page made me reel with excitement. Construction workers using backhoes and other heavy digging machinery on the banks of the James River in downtown Richmond had unearthed three boats dating back to the early 1800's.

According to the news story, the boats were buried in silt in an area that now was in the heart of the city, but that once was a turning basin and unloading point for water craft that floated down the James River and the Kanawha Canal to Richmond. The excavating, which was being done for what eventually would be office skyscrapers and a parking garage, had been halted while archaeologists studied the find.

My eyes raced over the newspaper description of the discovery. Two were wooden cargo boats called bateaux, measuring sixty-feet long, the article continued. Each would have carried a three-man crew, one man to steer into the current and the others to propel the boat with poles, while horses or mules walked on land beside the canal, pulling the vessels. The third boat was called a "packet boat," and was used for transporting passengers. It was forty-eight feet in length, wooden but with a metal hull.

I studied the pictures that appeared to have been taken from above, either from a helicopter, or perhaps the photographer had climbed to the top of a crane, or another big machine, and focused his camera on the hole in the ground where the ships were discovered. The curved wooden ribs of the boats were outlined in the mud, and there was no mistaking the shapes. I almost had the sensation of looking at the skeletons of some unknown animals.

That thought triggered my mind back to the day, months before, when Mrs. Holmes told students in my history class to write papers on cities. My grade was lower than I expected because I chose Richmond, but when referring to the city's history, I failed to mention the Kanawha Canal. I hadn't given that canal a thought since. The Kanawha hadn't been used in the twentieth century, and I suppose I took what was left of it for granted. When I stared at the newspaper pictures, it dawned on me that here was history right under my nose. I'd seen remnants of the canal locks when we crossed one of the bridges spanning the James River, and never paid attention to them.

"Dad, did you see this?" I held up the

newspaper, pointing to the pictures.

"Interesting, isn't it?" he replied. "The archaeologists will have a field day. But they have a tough task ahead of them — getting those boats out and trying to preserve them."

"*Trying* to preserve them?" I gave him a startled look. "If the boats have lasted more than a hundred and fifty years — "

"Yes, but they were buried in mud, Beth-Ann, away from air. Once the air hits them and that wood dries, they may disintegrate in a hurry."

"Can't they be saved?"

"I'm not up on the various preservation techniques. I don't know if the wood could be painted with some sort of resin, or whether the boats will have to be submerged in chemical baths until they soak up enough to keep them from deteriorating. The professional archaeologists probably know, and there must be a lot of people knowledgeable about that sort of thing at the Navy base, and at the shipyards of Norfolk and Newport News. That's just two hours from Richmond, so I don't doubt a lot of effort will be made to save the boats."

"Dad." I crossed the living room, and took a seat on the arm of his chair. "I want to see those boats. The place where they were found is right in the middle of Richmond, not very far from the capitol, so it shouldn't be hard to reach. Do you think we could go?"

"I'd like a look, too," he said. "We'll ride

over there sometime during the weekend if you want."

I gave him a hug.

After I was in bed that night I thought about Tony Roberts. As history-minded as Tony was, he'd be interested in the boats.

Mom and Dad were already in their room, and the house was dark when I crawled out of bed and padded into the living room. A street light outside the window illuminated a path for me, and I found the newspaper on the coffee table where I'd left it. I would save the article and pictures for Tony, I decided, and slipped back into bed once more. Maybe he'd come to Richmond soon and I would have a chance to show the paper to him . . . maybe.

Since my dates with Whit, I hadn't thought of Tony as often as I did immediately after meeting him. But I definitely hadn't forgotten him, or lost the desire to know him better. Closing my eyes, I had a mental picture of the way he looked as he sat on the Cantrells' sofa. I remembered how his left eyebrow lifted slightly when he smiled and how white his teeth were. He and I had had a great time that evening, and from what his sister said later, he seemed to like me.

But I hadn't heard from him. Rolling over, I told myself for the hundredth time that I was stupid to waste thoughts on a boy who probably had forgotten I existed.

Friday morning Mrs. Holmes devoted the

entire history class to the discovery of the boats, and the early importance of the Kanawha Canal. As Fran remarked afterwards, we were supposed to be studying World War II, instead we were back in the eighteenth and nineteenth centuries.

Mrs. Holmes said the original idea behind the canal was to connect the big ocean port of Hampton Roads with the west, all the way to the Rocky Mountains. While the James River was navigable from the Atlantic as far inland as Richmond, the seven miles of falls just past the city kept boats from continuing. The canal was started in the eighteenth century by the James River Company, headed by George Washington. By the mid-1800's it had been extended, so that transportation by water was possible 197 miles inland from the coast. Some of the Richmond locks were preserved, she added, even though the lock gates, which were made of wood, had rotted. The canal had been in constant use until the railroads were built.

I listened avidly, entranced with what Mrs. Holmes was saying. Not everybody in the class was interested. I glanced at Kenny Chapman and knew his mind was a million miles away. He sat sprawled in his chair, his legs stretched into the aisle, his face turned toward the window. I'd have bet any amount he'd tuned Mrs. Holmes out. History was a subject he took because it was required for a diploma; he had made it very plain to me he couldn't care less about the past.

F ifteen

My weekend included a variety of activities beginning with the trip to Monty's, and ending Sunday evening with an unexpected date. There was also some equally unexpected action on my part that took place on Friday afternoon.

While I was dressing to go to the pizza restaurant with Whit, Mrs. Cantrell phoned to ask if I'd baby-sit with her children at seven o'clock. After explaining that I had personal plans for the evening, she sounded so wistful at my refusal that I mentioned being available for Saturday night.

"Really? That's unbelievable, Beth-Ann. Please stay with my children then. Richard and I don't have any specific plans for tonight and delaying twenty-four hours won't matter. But both of us do need an evening out. I never dared to hope you wouldn't be dating on a Saturday night."

"I'll be there tomorrow. I — Mrs. Cantrell — " I caught my breath, the unspoken words burning in my mouth. "Have you seen or heard about finding the buried boats in the basin of the Kanawha Canal? I've saved the newspaper clippings and thought — I mean — " my tongue moved across incredibly dry lips " — I thought your brother might be interested, since he's involved in an archaeological dig, but I don't have a mailing address for him."

I spoke so rapidly the syllables ran together, as if what I uttered was one long word. The remarks weren't planned; they simply popped out because talking to her made my feelings for Tony acute. I'd been thinking about him off and on all day.

"I'm sure he'll be delighted," she said. "You're a dear to remember that he's a history buff. Here's the address."

I wrote down what she dictated, amazed at asking for it. I didn't want her to know how much I was drawn to Tony. My old shyness about making overtures to boys was resurfacing, I guess. But it would be easier to bear Tony's ignoring me if it was my secret.

Whit was knocking on our front door when I told Mrs. Cantrell good-bye.

Something I'd been dreading happened at Monty's that night — I came face to face with Kenny, in a situation where he and I couldn't ignore each other.

Vicki and Chris were already in the

restaurant at a table for four when Whit and I arrived. Every seat was taken except the two they'd saved for us. "This place is jammed on weekends, so we came a few minutes early to find a table without having to wait," Chris explained. "I'm getting hungrier by the minute from smelling the pizza. Let's order right away."

The May weather was so warm that summer clothes were in evidence. Vicki looked darling in a long-sleeved, pale green cotton dress. I was glad I'd worn my yellow linen skirt with a yellow- and white-striped blouse instead of jeans. There were times when I particularly wanted to appear feminine and that evening was one, although I wasn't sure why. It might have been because I was with Whit, who always looked nice. I wasn't in love with Whit, as I'd once thought I was with Kenny, but I enjoyed being with him, and the same feelings were true about being with Vicki and Chris.

We'd almost finished eating when Kenny came in with Katie Wells. They skirted the line waiting for seats and ambled over to us. We might have crowded one person in, but the tables were small, and we were in a corner. There wasn't room for two more chairs.

"Hi, people," Kenny said, his eyes moving around the table. When his gaze reached me I forced a smile and gave an answering hello, refusing to look in another direction until after he did. It was the first time he and I had made eye contact since our quarrel.

Katie, who was the bubbly type, began chatting at once. She wanted to know what kinds of pizza we'd ordered, and how long we had to wait for service, and who we'd seen from school. She didn't pause to give anyone a chance to answer, and finally Kenny interrupted her to announce that they were going to the movies after they ate.

"Want to come along?" His eyes circled our group once more.

To my relief, none of our foursome bought the idea. "Some other night," Chris replied. "We're going to Vicki's to play Trivial Pursuit. Why don't you two join us?"

That was the first I'd heard of finishing the evening at Vicki's, but it suited me. Kenny glanced expectantly toward his date. I decided he wanted to go to Vicki's, but Katie shook her head.

"I really want to see that movie," she told him. She actually looked as if she might cry.

They left us to get in the line waiting for tables. I wasn't aware of holding my breath until I gulped air, very glad they wouldn't come to Vicki's house. I could now cope with being in the same room with Kenny, but it might take the edge off my fun. Kenny, who hadn't wanted me to make a single suggestion about what he and I did on dates, had bowed instantly to Katie's whim, which made me wonder if the two of them were becoming serious, or if she'd managed to coax him into whatever she wanted. It didn't seem important, an indication to me that I truly had succeeded in getting over Kenny Chapman.

When Whit drove me home it was almost midnight.

"Wish me luck with my job tomorrow, Beth-Ann," Whit said as we reached my house, and he turned off the ignition.

"You won't need luck. You already know the ropes, since you worked in that hardware store during the Christmas holidays."

"But with new owners, that means a new boss. Probably new rules, too."

He barely finished the sentence before leaning across the car seat to kiss me on the mouth. I hadn't anticipated it, but I responded, my lips tingling under his.

"I was afraid if we waited until we were at your door with that outside light blazing down on us, a good-night kiss might be out of reach," he murmured, and he leaned across the seat to kiss me again.

His arm was around my shoulders as we left the car and walked to the house, and I vowed silently to replace Mom's big bulb with a much smaller one before another date brought me home.

Instead of sleeping late Saturday, as I did most weekends, I was up before my parents. I had a project. Writing Tony was my first priority of the day, and I wanted the letter in the mail early in the hope that it would reach him Monday. If he answered by return mail. . . . Thinking about it made me smile. Please, Tony, I thought. Please.

More news stories and pictures of the boats had been in the Friday morning paper and I'd saved all of them, but I didn't want to send just the clippings. A letter would make it more personal, but writing even two or three paragraphs turned out to be harder than I anticipated.

My best stationery was pale blue, with my initials printed in darker blue ink. After messing up four sheets, I decided to do a rough draft on notebook paper and recopy it. At the rate I was going, I might use up the entire box of blue paper before the letter was to my liking.

The final results didn't materialize until after Mom had made breakfast for Dad and me. I returned to my room and worked another hour before settling for sentences that seemed disjointed, but I didn't think I could improve on them. In case Tony had forgotten me, I wanted to mention the Cantrells to jog his memory, and signing "Sincerely," seemed trite. Still, it was better than, "Yours truly," or, "Your friend."

Dear Tony,

As you can see by the enclosed clippings, Richmond now has an archaeological dig just like Williamsburg.

Dad and I are going to downtown Richmond this morning to have a look at the boats.

Tonight I'll tell Tessa and Timmy about them when I'm baby-sitting there.

I hope you finished your senior thesis and got an A.

Sincerely,
Beth-Ann Hughes

In the middle of the morning, Dad asked if I was ready for what he called "our boat excursion," and I said yes. The letter was addressed and stamped. We would pass a branch post office on our way and the sooner I mailed it, the sooner it would reach Tony in northern Virginia.

A rope barricade had been put up around the area where the boats were found, and Dad and I joined some fifty or sixty people who were looking into the hole that eventually would be the basement and sub-basement of the building to be constructed. I could see the outline of the boats; their shapes appeared just as they had in the newspaper pictures. Another group worked in the mud below, carefully scraping silt and grime off pieces of wood. Bright sunshine was already drying the mud to a crust in some spots.

A man in a hard hat that seemed oddly out of place with his white shirt and necktie stood beside my father, and they struck up a conversation. It turned out the man was one of the construction company supervisors, and he was there out of curiosity rather than being on duty.

"I put on my hard hat out of habit when I'm at a building site," he explained. "We've called a halt to our work until the boats can be moved. I don't know how long that will be. A couple of weeks, at the earliest, but we can't delay indefinitely, since there's a deadline for completion of the building."

"It looks as if the people down in the hole are breaking up some of the boat ribs," Dad commented. I'd wondered about that, too.

"There's no way to lift the larger boats out in one piece, because the wood is too fragile," the supervisor said. "The parts are being moved separately and numbered so the boats can be reconstructed. A local firm is donating use of a Fiberglas fuel tank where the wood can be submerged in polyethylene glycol, which is a water-soluble resin."

Dad inquired about the people in the hole. It seemed they were members of a historical organization along with some trained archaeologists. The man in the hard hat remarked that the backhoe operator deserved a lot of credit.

"He stopped excavating when he realized he'd unearthed more than junk. Other outfits have pitched in, too. Several private organizations and businesses are donating equipment and time to save the boats," he said.

The morning was unseasonably hot for May, but even though the sun bore down, Dad and I lingered until noon. As we headed home, we talked about the find and what we'd seen.

"I didn't realize you were so interested in history," I told him.

"I didn't, either," he came back with a smile. "After all, though, we live in a very historic city in a very historic state. Maybe all of us should be more aware of it."

He was describing exactly the way I felt.

That afternoon I walked to Fran's, wearing my bathing suit under shorts and a knitted shirt. She'd called to suggest that we sit in her backyard to get the beginnings of a summer tan. I thought it was a super idea, even though I knew I'd have to watch myself. Fran browned into a beautiful golden color, while my skin was fair and if I wasn't careful about acquiring a tan gradually, I'd be as red as a ripe tomato.

She mixed up a pitcher of lemonade, and we stretched out on beach towels on the grass, gabbing, but not talking about earthshaking matters. After an hour I moved into the shade with my legs still in the sunshine. The chitchat turned to boys; she had a date with Jack that night, of course. When I said I was baby-sitting, she scowled.

"Ugh, Beth-Ann. How gross," she said. "On Saturday night, too. That's not for me."

"I had a date, and a great time last night," I reminded her, thinking secretly that my Saturday baby-sitting might turn into a date after all. If Tony was spending this sunny Saturday in Williamsburg . . . and if he decided to stay overnight at his sister's. . . .

"Why are you smiling?" she asked. "Let me in on the joke."

"No reason." I wouldn't have admitted for anything that thinking about a certain boy made me smile. "It's a beautiful day and I feel good. So, why not smile?"

"Why not?" Apparently she was satisfied with my evasive answer, and she changed the subject, describing a cute black and white linen dress she'd seen in a shop window. It was her size and she'd tried it on, finding it a perfect fit, but the price was prohibitive.

"Mom says if she buys that little number for me, I won't get any other new clothes until fall," she said with a shrug. "So, it's still in the store."

Tony didn't come to the Cantrells that night. It was a routine evening for me as I fought disappointment, telling myself I'd had no reason to expect him. I played with Tessa and Timmy, put them to bed, and watched a TV movie until Mr. and Mrs. Cantrell returned home.

My second surprise of the weekend — the first was finding courage to write Tony — came late Sunday afternoon when Chris Abernathy asked me for a date.

It was another rainy Sunday. We'd had our share of those during the spring, I thought ruefully as I stood at the living room window and watched water cascading down the glass panes. I read the comics in the Sunday paper and turned to the feature section, not finding

165

much of interest. Mom and Dad were taking naps and I glanced at the rain once more, wishing driver's ed was a thing of the past, and that I had my license and could go somewhere in the car. That was my state of mind when Chris phoned.

"I bumped into Kenny this morning and he said the movie he and Katie saw Friday night is fantastic," he said. "Want to give it a try tonight, Beth-Ann?"

Chris Abernathy was asking *me* for a date! A wave of excitement washed over me. I'd never said more than a few hellos to him until Friday night at Monty's and at Vicki's.

"Love to," I answered. The two words had a happy sound.

To some girls, the invitation might not have seemed like a big deal, but it was a fresh thrill every time I heard from a boy. I suppose I was still such a novice at dating that it was difficult to believe the good things coming my way.

Chris and I agreed with Kenny about the movie. It was a thriller that kept us in suspense until the very end. When we left the theater, we stopped at a drive-in for Cokes, and a little later as my house came into view with its outside light glowing, I realized I'd neglected to swap Mom's big bulb for a small one.

It wasn't vital at the moment because I didn't feel Chris and I would share any goodnight kisses, not on a first date. I was correct.

........................letter..............
....

Sixteen

When you want something to happen and it doesn't, time has a way of inching along hopelessly. I thought I might hear from Tony in Tuesday's mail, if he wrote me the instant my letter arrived, but I didn't. On Wednesday afternoon I rushed home from the driver's ed class, anxious to get to the mailbox, and had to stifle my disappointment again. There were two letters for Dad, both of them looking like bills, and Mom had a magazine. I didn't get anything.

Don't hope — don't hope — don't hope, I told myself, repeating the words as if they were the refrain of a song. But I did hope, and Thursday's disappointment was a hurtful blow. The waiting and wanting were taking their toll on my disposition, and at school I kept to myself. No wonder I didn't have any weekend dates lined up, I reflected. My glumness had to be showing.

Mom was cooking fish for dinner Friday night and I was chopping lettuce, tomatoes, and cucumbers for a salad when the phone rang. I went to my room to answer. I was flabbergasted that it was a person-to-person long distance call for me, I'd never received that sort of phone call in my life.

"Beth-Ann" — it was Tony's voice and my knees began to wobble — "I received your letter and clippings, and they made my day. I want you to know how glad I am to have them."

"I'm glad you're glad." I nearly choked — that had to be the corniest remark of the century.

"Have you had a chance to see the boats yet? Your letter said you might do it last Saturday."

I described Dad's and my "boat excursion" in a voice that continued to quiver.

"Beth-Ann, you seem so interested in the dig that I wondered if you'd like to come to Williamsburg with me Saturday. That is, if you don't mind getting your hands dirty. I've contacted Rex, the archaeologist, and he says it's okay for me to bring you, although they're winding up the dig, and tomorrow will be the final day. You won't be paid. I'm not paid, either, but if you'd enjoy — "

"I would!" I didn't let him finish. "Tony, you don't know how great that will be!"

"It won't mess up your weekend plans to give you such short notice?"

I almost said I didn't have weekend plans,

but caught myself. "This is the best weekend plan I could possibly have," I told him.

"I haven't been to Williamsburg in quite a while and I hate for the dig to end, but there was stuff here I had to do on Saturdays. My thesis first, and after that, I had to take a four-week first aid course on Saturdays since I'll be senior lifeguard at the pool this summer. That's why you haven't seen me recently."

"I've missed you." I couldn't believe I said it.

"You mean that, Beth-Ann?"

"Very much."

"Margaret told me you dated every weekend, so I didn't know if you were involved with some special guy or — or something."

"I'm not."

"Gosh, you don't know what a relief that is!"

Both of us laughed.

"We need to get an early start tomorrow," he went on. "Can you be ready at six in the morning?"

"Earlier than that if you want."

"Six is soon enough for me," he chuckled. "Wear your old clothes because you'll be scrambling around in the dirt. I'm coming to Richmond tonight, but it probably will be late before I reach Margaret's, so I'll see you tomorrow. Incidentally, if you're free Sunday, you can show me your boats."

I told him I'd look forward to it, and we

exchanged good-byes. I stared at the phone a long time after we hung up, trying to get my breathing back to normal. I was beaming when I returned to the kitchen to tell Mom I had marvelous weekend plans.

Saturday was a glorious sun-washed day. I was sitting on our front steps, waiting, when Tony came out of the Cantrells' house. While I thought I had remembered everything about him, I must have forgotten how handsome he was. We smiled at each other a little shyly without saying much for a few minutes, then both of us began talking at once.

We reached the Williamsburg dig an hour later to find several people hard at work in ground that had been divided into grids by strings.

"We'll work here," Tony said, pointing to a small square. After he introduced me to Rex, a red-haired man with a short, red beard, he said, "You sift through the dirt with a garden trowel, or a spoon, or your hands."

If that day had been measured by what we found, I suppose it would have been classified as a failure. Tony found a few shards, chips of broken pottery. I didn't come across anything until late afternoon when I unearthed a corroded stick about two inches long that Rex said was possibly part of a broken nail, since it was metal. I measured the day in fun, not in achievements, and it was fantastic. I was with Tony, stooping down beside him, and it didn't matter that my back was tired, or that my face and clothes were smudged with dirt.

We left Williamsburg at twilight, and it was dark by the time Tony stopped in front of his sister's house.

"Tired?" he asked.

"A little. But it's a good tired." I smiled at him. There was enough light coming through the automobile windows for me to make out his features.

"Want to see if we can find some hamburgers, Beth-Ann?"

"I certainly would — after I have a shower." Our lunch of peanut butter crackers seemed a long time ago. "I can't go any place looking like this."

"Oh, I don't think you look that awful. But then, I'm not exactly Mr. Clean at the moment, myself. I know what you mean about wanting a shower. Are you a fast dresser or a slow one?"

"Medium fast," I replied in a teasing voice. "What about you?"

"Real fast at times. Suppose I ring your doorbell in fifteen minutes?"

I nodded and put my hand on the door handle, ready to leave the car, when he stopped me.

"Wait a sec," he said softly. "I just want you to know how much fun I've had with you today. There's something I haven't told you. Next fall I'll be in college in Williamsburg —

at William and Mary. That means you and I can see a lot of each other, if that's okay with you."

My heart was pounding. "It's very okay," I said. In the dimness of the car I realized he was looking at my mouth, and I knew he wanted to kiss me, and I wanted that kiss. I leaned toward him just a little. The kiss was gentle and sweet — very, very sweet.

"That's just the beginning, Beth-Ann," he said softly. "After we get cleaned up, we can pick up where we left off."

Looking at him, I laughed, happier than I'd ever been in my life. I wouldn't see Tony just this one weekend; he wanted to be with me as much as I longed to be with him.

"Look, you're smiling," he said as he walked across the street with me to my house. We were holding hands.

"I know." My smile grew wider. "That's because the day has been so wonderful and I'm so happy and — " I broke the sentence off, not knowing what to say next.

Tony understood. He squeezed my hand and looked right into my eyes. "I may be ringing your bell sooner than fifteen minutes," he announced. "Maybe twelve or thirteen minutes. I can't wait fifteen minutes before seeing you again."